EAR
CONVERSATIONALIST

"*The Conversationalist* is a brilliant example of modern American literature. It is a haunting tale about the destructive path of tragedy; and how emotional scars can continue long after the event as people go through the motions of trying to move on, and do what is *expected*."—M.E. Franco, author of **The Dion Series** and **The Rustler's Daughter**

"This novella masters the character of the hero in a way that reminded me of what was best about the novels of John Updike, to name one example. Justin Bog captures this character so well that I felt like I was walking around in his shoes. It is nice to see a master craftsman at work."—Stacey Roberts, author of **Trailer Trash, with a Girl's Name**

"Blown the freak away: My rather mind-boggled trip into the realm of Bogville this second time around has left me almost speechless. His ability to delve so deeply and darkly into the corners some folks dare not venture, and with such a gentle touch, can only be compared to that of a skilled surgeon. But instead of a scalpel, he wields a quill."—Kriss Morton, of **cabingoddess.com**

"The Conversationalist pulled me in, then the twist took me by surprise. Justin Bog writes characters that could be any one of us."—Toni Rakestraw, co-author of **Titanic Deception**

"Bog creates worlds that don't merely scratch the surface. We plunge deep into the minds and wants of his characters. We come to know them—and their hearts' desires."—Jason McIntyre, author of **On the Gathering Storm** and **The Devil's Right Hand**

"*The Conversationalist* is set in the San Juan Islands with the basic theme of modern day dating scene. Patrick is the odd one out in the town and everyone thinks that there is something wrong with him . . . Justin Bog delves right into these aspects through Patrick, the oddball and Wendy, the woman obsessed with death. It is difficult to discuss the plot without giving out spoilers and so all I will say about it is that it is nothing like anything that you can guess. It is different and twisted and has a magnetic quality to it that keeps the reader turning its very few pages. And yeah, that is another quality that I admire about this author. He tells us all his fascinating stories using minimal words and yet creates an effect that even very complicated novels can fail in creating. As I turned (or swiped on my kindle) to the last page, I felt like I was in a trance that broke with the blank space at the end of the book . . . When I first read Justin Bog's *Sandcastle and Other Stories*, I was taken aback by his dark themes and gritty writing style. As I re-read a few of the stories from *Sandcastle* before picking up this one, I felt that I was more ready for what was to come. Yet I was taken by surprise once again. Almost like standing on a train track and waiting for a train to make it through the last bend, and then all of a sudden it is just there. I don't have words for the experience that this book brings with – you have to experience it for yourself! So don't wait – just pick it up . . . NOW!"—book r3vi3ws

"In *The Conversationalist*, words flow like calm waters, lulling readers into a false sense of security. The plot builds and we are forced to ride the wave, unknowing of where it might take us. Juxtaposing an underlying tension with prose is where Mr. Bog's writing shines. He invites us to plunge into darkness with his characters, and we go willingly. This is the mark of a talented and fearless storyteller." —Eden Baylee is the author of several erotic anthologies, including **Spring into Summer**. Her forthcoming, yet-to-be-named novel is a psychological, erotic thriller.

"Justin Bog excels at creating worlds inside the human condition; he shines a bright light on the dark places we all contain but rarely visit. Don't miss *The Conversationalist*—a perfect example of the lives inside his head. And now, inside ours."— Rachel Thompson, author of **A Walk in the Snark** and **Broken Pieces**

"This novella creeps into a rising tension that builds throughout the piece, gathering a slow power that hits squarely in the last chapter to masterful effect . . . The quiet descriptive passages and almost whisper soft demeanor of the narrator hide the suspense as the chapters progress. I found myself entranced and unable to stop reading, as if this book were an action thriller instead of an intense character study . . . Justin possesses an uncanny ability with words that evokes powerful imagery without slowing the tempo or suspense in this novella . . . I highly recommend this book to all that want a deeper experience with their fiction. This one will make you think and ponder for long after the last page is read."—Stephen Moran, author of **Ella**

WHAT READERS HAVE SAID ABOUT THE WRITING OF JUSTIN BOG

"Justin Bog's first collection of short stories, **Sandcastle and Other Stories**, works brilliantly on many levels. Bog's prose is stark and lean, and he excels at description. He is a keen observer of life and people, and through his characters, he skims painfully close to thoughts, feelings, and behaviors that could belong to any of us."—Gae-Lynn Woods, author of **The Devil of Light** and the newly released sequel, **Avengers of Blood (A Cass Elliot Crime Novel)**

"(**Sandcastle and Other Stories**) is a wonderful collection of short stories. The stories don't have a common theme running through them, but one thing that is common throughout is the way the author is able to introduce many diverse characters and yet make the reader feel as though he or she is looking at the world through the eyes of the character; really getting inside that character's mind and getting a feeling for the emotions. The quality of the description and the obvious talent the author has to be able to observe and recount different aspects of human behavior is exceptional."—Maria Savva, author of **Haunted** and **Fusion**

BOOKS BY JUSTIN BOG

Novel

Wake Me Up

Collections

Hark: A Christmas Collection
Sandcastle and Other Stories
Speak the Word

HORRORSTRUCK NOVELLA ONE

THE CONVERSATIONALIST

JUSTIN BOG

The Author's Advocate

Dedicated with love, laughter, and affection to my three Ellison nephews: Max, Lucas, and Jackson James!

CONTENTS

FOREWORD

BY RACHEL THOMPSON

I'm always chatting with authors—I love writing and reading. What drives us? What fascinates us? Why do we write?

I'm grateful to be involved in such a creative community. Every single day I find someone new I want to share with the world.

So, I couldn't be more thrilled to present Justin Bog to you. His well-crafted first collection of literary psychological tales, Sandcastle and Other Stories, stays in my reread file—please find a copy right now and fall, as I did, into the dark situations Bog created.

Now, with The Conversationalist (and any compelling story) there's a certain amount of craft, and that's what Justin Bog does so well—he is a born writer. When I read his work, I'm amazed at how lyrical it is; that's such a talent. Here's one of my favorite passages:

Now, a month later, I sit, foggy, a similar state of mind, in a different seafood restaurant with a locals-know-every-secret bar, two happy hour martinis downed, fidgeting with my napkin below the lip of the table, and I barely hear Wendy ask me another question. She brought a bag of them tonight.

Let me back up a bit.

I met Justin online months before he published Sandcastle and Other Stories, and it was as if I'd found the sweet, kind, intelligent brother I never got to have (to clarify, I have no brothers). We fell into an easy camaraderie discussing our writing lives, as Justin refers to it. We gave each other critiques on writing for our upcoming books; his talent shines, and his incredibly generous nature, particularly toward other authors and creative, inspires.

Justin was eager to understand more about marketing his book, even though it wasn't due out for another six months or so. Which is smart. (In my role as consultant for the company I founded, BadRedhead Media, I see too many authors wanting to start the process *after* their book release.) Many authors fear marketing a book they haven't released yet, but that's when you must start to build up an author platform.

Six months later, guess what happened? Within a few days of release, Sandcastle and Other Stories was ranked in the Top 100 Paid on several key bestseller lists at Amazon. We were thrilled!

Even better? Three weeks before the release, a publishing house (in his home state of Washington) made contact to discuss signing him for this book and future works! The publisher had been reading Justin's writing on his blog, and following his progress through Social Media—the author platform worked. Every author's dream had come true.

I'm so thrilled to watch a talented author receive such encouragement (and rave reviews along the way), and, even more importantly, secure a writing future. As you discover Sandcastle and Other Stories, I highly suggest you read each tale slowly; savor every carefully selected word, phrase, and meaning. Justin takes you on a psychological ride that may even make you uncomfortable during some shocking moments, and in that way, he succeeds on an entirely different level than strictly entertainment: he makes you feel something—the mark of a truly gifted author.

Once you're done with this book, you'll want to read it again. And again. And then you'll want more. And here it is: enjoy The Conversationalist.

Now, I cannot wait for Justin Bog's next book; I bet you won't be able to either.

Rachel Thompson

Author (Broken Pieces, A Walk In The Snark and The Mancode: Exposed; social media, branding, and book specialist at BadRedhead Media)

THE CONVERSATIONALIST

1

Wendy sits across from me and tells me she's afraid to die. She wonders what it's like.

"What if *this* is all there is?" she says.

It isn't easy for me to listen to the words Wendy speaks. My index finger traces through the condensation at the base of my martini glass as her forlorn questioning waves hit me. I don't repeat to her out loud her last yearning words in a combative tone. I want to. Inside, thoughts about life, death, endings, unfairness turned to bitterness, propagate.

"My mother died a year ago," she says, lowering her voice as she glances at the diners around us, "horribly." I don't know Wendy well enough to understand if she's embarrassed by her own boldness, revealing a personal lament right out in the open, or by her mother's ill fortune.

I watch her lips move, opening, pressing tightly together then opening again, sipping hot coffee. She didn't add anything sweet to hers.

There's a catch in Wendy's voice when she finishes her story, as if something keeps snagging on a hook down her throat. I hope the coffee soothes her ache.

"You'll soon come to a point when you realize you need to move on with your life, right? I mean, you're always going to grieve," I say. "It's over now. Think about what your mother would want you to do." I let her see nothing but understanding, a melancholy concentration, on my face, while inside I'm perplexed, a sweating liar. The image of my own mother tries to surface and it takes all I have to stifle her visage from taking over my every thought. I can't help but remember, at this stressed moment, the whip of my mother's slashing smile, an icy thing that belonged in deep waters, hidden away in darkness.

"I keep thinking about train accidents," Wendy says. She lifts a pale hand to her cheek and brushes a loose strand of hair away. "And how stupid they are."

I nod my head and try to listen. All I see now is my mother's smile turning to a downturned, besmirched, frown, how quick her unpleasant countenance turned into a scowl. I would flee the room, the home, walk, run away to the cliff-side pathways, meander for hours until safe to sneak back . . . mother in a gin-fueled stupor, now passed out and harmless.

Wendy isn't a mind reader. She sees only steady concern, and this is too easy for me to pull off.

"How awful," I say, "no one thinks of trains anymore, even when they rush right through Seattle and northward, hugging the coastline. They stop us when we least expect it." And this isn't the right thing to say either. I can see Wendy coming to the same conclusion, and I ask her if she'd like to change the subject.

Only a month ago, Wendy, a friend of an acquaintance, took me into her confidence, or wanted to place me in that position: noble listener—I found it all a bit desperate. On our first date I drove her to a quiet, secluded dinner at The Chuckanut Manor, a family-run establishment looking out over the oyster-rich waters of Puget

Sound. Once seated and waiting for a very dry martini (no vermouth and lots of blue-cheese-stuffed olives), I'd need at least two just to settle into a functioning haze, a single glass of Mellisoni Vineyard's award-winning Pinot Grigio for Wendy, gulf prawn and avocado cocktails to start, she allowed me to prattle on about my cat, Roadway, who needed an operation on her kidney, and how much it would cost; let me ask her what she would do: pay the horrendous and expensive bill or acquiesce to Roadway becoming road kill. She listened to my sorry tale; it's where my mind was at on that day.

Now, this Friday, almost a month later, I sit, foggy, a similar state of mind, in a different seafood restaurant with a locals-know-every-secret bar, two happy hour martinis downed, fidgeting with my napkin below the lip of the table, and I barely hear Wendy ask me another question. She brought a bag of them tonight.

"Do you know how she died?" I can only concentrate on Roadway, my mournful pussycat's howl of pain echoing. She finally had the necessary surgery, and rests this very moment at home with a shaved and sutured belly, still dazed and resentful from the anesthetic. I didn't even want to leave her but my cat isn't going anywhere. Online, I'd been reading horror stories about vets and how some give too much happy gas, so to speak, and the pets never wake up, how the same vets have to tell the owners what happened, and how many of them lie with ease.

I cannot, for the life of me, figure out why I called Wendy to see her again—we didn't have any spark, only a fondness for relating to despair and how the world loved to kick anyone down right when the ship sets sail on a maiden voyage, champagne bottle breaking during a bubbly christening. Here's our family at our happiest. And that moment? Decades ago now. I shake this memory away with fierce inner urgency.

Why did I need to see Wendy again tonight? Or two weeks ago when we met each other at the local cinema for a movie all the most trenchant critics compared favorably to the best Woody Allen flicks—a bit of human companionship, over and done with. Not a lot of time to talk during a movie, and I had to get up early to teach. Maybe I reached my loneliness limit and (settling) called Wendy to prove to myself that I could interact with another person in a selfless manner—it's a test I failed, and this defeat is there in the pit of my stomach even now—but, at that point in time, Roadway's surgery date dinged from my phone's appointment reminder. I'd been saving my extra cash to give to the vet.

"No, but when anyone dies, or anything, it must hurt." I want to change the subject—I resist the urge to glance at my iPhone to check the time. I no longer wear a watch, but I've been contemplating the iWatch to aid in this kind of maneuver, being present while not being present.

The late afternoon happy hour dinner date began with a walk along the docks—economizing. Wendy even spotted a couple fat and sleek sea otters in the far distance, shuffling about the end of one of the dock lanes. I tried to get closer but they're shy little buggers and these crafty swift otters slunk into the water and that was that—the night's excitement. Then Wendy and I walked over to Anthony's, a wish-you-could-eat-the-view seafood restaurant overlooking the very same

Anacortes marina docks. There's another marina on the other side of Fidalgo Island, closer to where I live, where my parents' summer cottage sits on a ridge next to State park land. I can't focus on anything Wendy says, her gloomy tone, and there won't be another date. I can tell you that much right now.

"What are your weekend plans?" I say, a conversation starter as weightless as the opening joke from an insincere comic.

"I'm not sure. Most of my hours will be filled with planning for a new project. I'd tell you more, but I don't want to jinx it. Weren't those otters the cutest?"

"Yes. It's rare to see them. I've lived here so long but I've only run across them a few times." A waitress passes by. She's carrying a tray filled with fish & chips, grass fed burgers, and Asian salads. The clink of cutlery against plates is unnerving. It's not the quietest of restaurants, and I almost can't hear Wendy's words, and that adds to my impatience—it's my chore to listen, be attentive, give meaning to the smallest of details she's sharing.

I want to keep my mind off the glistening fish being passed around, steaming, because that thought will lead to where the salmon is caught, and how much toxicity spreads into The Sound each year—the radiation from that Japanese nuclear accident has reached our waters, and I believe all Pacific fish are now tainted, the other mammals, the bears searching under rocks for crab, our cute little otters, suffering from the tiniest bit of radiation poisoning, skin lesions, finally drowning. Talking about death, the event and afterwards, makes me want to ask the waiter how the shrimps and mussels are packed; are they on ice and kept fresh in the open kitchen storage bins?

"She was hit by a train," Wendy says. "I keep picturing my mother in her new car, one of those big luxury Lincolns matching the color of her fingernail polish—a bruised rose. She bought this new car and look what happens. I don't have the answers." She stares at me—right into my eyes. I can feel her reaching and diving as if she expects me to pull her to safety, away from the wreckage somehow, to pull her mother out of a hat like a cheap party magician's trick. "I can see her in *this car* she just had to have as the train comes closer. There was a time when I used to make fun of the stupidity. I mean, how could she stay in a car knowing a train is barreling towards her? Unless she wanted to."

"What did the police say, the investigation?" A busboy fills our water glasses. He does this too often, and I understand his boredom. I ask him to bring more coffee. The light tone of my voice pushes the conversation Wendy and I are having into the surreal. I read the local paper online at the office and I'm always startled to hear some poor soul has been killed by one of the trains—usually at a rural crossing in the farmland, the tulip fields. I always wonder why they couldn't flee the tracks, if some of them wanted an end like this to escape. It's usually in the wee hours of the morning. Work traffic is seldom stalled. "Wendy, do you want to talk about something else?"

She hasn't known me long enough to perceive how I change subjects frequently. I'm really trying with Wendy; maybe to prove I can. My sister, Jobeth, told me I act like a commercial for diet soda or a new music video, always trying to cram as much dancing, jingle, and information into that thirty second spot before switching to the next topic. She says I've turned into a sound bite—simply faking agreeability. "You need to become a better listener," she said. I remember Jobeth hanging the telephone up; angry at her husband, who told her he was leaving her for another woman, and angry with me because I couldn't listen to her even though I had the time. I called her seconds later, but she'd turned her answering machine on and I was sent straight to voicemail. I left her this message: *I'm sorry, Jo. You know me. I won't change the subject . . . I'm really listening. I love you. Call me back.*

Wendy sips her wine, and then says, "No. I have to tell you. We're just starting to get to know each other a bit better. I need to tell you." Out in the open, in front of every other person in the restaurant, I want to slap myself in the face and run from her—the getting-to-know-each-other-better line grates. I'm not an expert. I'm not a doctor anyone should run to for answers.

"Hold on, I see the waiter coming. One second." I've shushed her with a bit more than a little unconcealable frost. Wendy stands up, grasping her small black purse, and tells me she'll be right back. Her tone is neutral, plain as a waning moon. I wonder if I've offended her too much. It's what I do best. That's what Jobeth always says: *Unfortunately, you seem to have inherited Mother's tact, Patrick.* Jobeth meant the opposite, attaches a snarky twist on the word tact.

The waiter, after watching Wendy head to the restroom, veers off in a different direction, away from our table. I can think of many things to say to Wendy, but I only want to leave. I'll wake up in the morning without any energy, have the weekend to prepare to teach English at the Community College and answer, repeatedly, the simple questions from those students who forgot to write down my last assignment. I actually look forward to holing up in my office—I'm going to disappear this weekend, not that anyone else would notice.

It's one of those times when I see my actions from outside myself. I view my body from a distance as it gets up from the table, leaving enough money to cover both dinners, and then presses onward to the entry doors and out. In the early

evening dimming I find my car parked next to
Wendy's, who insisted she also drive so I wouldn't
have to rush through reverse-commute traffic after
my office hours. She's oppressively thoughtful.

I can't be in a situation like this. I need to break
from her cleanly. I've fooled myself into thinking
I'm not as lonely as I was a few months ago. I fell
into a fog, listening, by revealing more to a guy
from work I hung out with infrequently, accepting a
spontaneous "Want to grab a beer or two?" This
acquaintance, a drinking buddy, who, in his
inebriated state, wouldn't remember any trenchant
detail I offered from my own life, if only to be
polite—my monkish existence became a complaint,
and our conversation turned on alienation, his, my
own, his single status something he says he wished
for, another lie—I relished my weaker moment of
angst, a confession of loneliness given to another
teacher in the English Department over dark beer
at a local brewery in downtown Mount Vernon. My
colleague commiserated as much as he could, too
broken by a recent separation, and an antagonistic
ongoing divorce where his two kids had become
ping pong balls in a game with no score. When

drunk, he, with an insidious, vengeful tone accompanied by physical gestures better left forgotten, censored, went off on all women in the most loathsome misogynistic manner. He told me to avoid them like the plague, that I was lucky to be single, enjoy my time without the obligations.

"You don't have to compromise one shitty bit." He finished by tearing up, alcohol the best depressant, telling me how much he still loved his wife, that she'd found another guy (proud to spill her secret when he finally said, "I know something's off. You're not acting like yourself . . . what's bothering you? Is it me?" That she'd pursued this lover. I could see them rutting in a tire-scented office, grease and oil blotches blemishing his wife's freckled arms), a mechanic at a tire rotation place, someone, she said, who treated her like a woman should be treated—she justified her tawdry behavior by diminishing her husband, finding every excuse to shift blame, telling him he's a doormat, that she missed a spark. It's usually a third party, I replied, that breaks up any relationship, and not only the romantic ones. I drove him back to his new bachelor pad, a two-room shit heap behind the

Sports Keg in Burlington where the noise of the main commerce street becomes white noise hum.

As the engine rumbles in my old Toyota Highlander—please start—my mind is concentrating on trains, Wendy in the restroom trying to pull her frazzled grief stricken life together, and how memories can control emotions too much. I won't let mine do that. There's nothing wrong with what I'm doing. By the time I get home, I've convinced myself of that fact.

2

On Monday morning, after a weekend filled
with too much solitary drinking, something I try to
keep quiet about, I wake up fast, cut the alarm clock
buzz short, with the egged-up feeling of hangover
prominent amidst a refreshing clearness of
purpose—who can fathom why the mind allows for
such dichotomy—even after all the booze at the
restaurant, and a big glass of Knob Creek before
bed to knock the cacophony of dreary thoughts to
dust. I repeat the Knob Creek on Saturday and
Sunday evenings, and need a new bottle. It's a vice I
can afford on my teaching salary.

My head is a knot: it feels twisted and reshaped
during sleep. When I look in the mirror I can
picture the tracks of rope tightening around my
brain—Wendy's words linger—tightening them.
Normally, I try to be an optimist, and I know how
hard that is for anyone around me to believe but I
love the sunnier side of the street, pop songs,
carnivals, Sally Field movies where she eventually
rises above the made-up situation with pugnacious

dignity (I do know that's most of her film oeuvre); I rely on the struggle to remain positive to shape my worldview. Otherwise, cynicism brings me lower than any other feeling—like it wants to do this morning.

Wendy returns; now she haunts me while I sleep. Dreams strive to sway my judgment when I awake. I picture train crashes as fantastic destruction, fast, sparks, a metal Armageddon, but when going slowly, they can cause just as much damage. As I splash water on my face I realize it was Wendy, once again sitting across from me in my dream—waiters with bored expressions stretched in caricature interrupting with steady frequency—with her mouth twitching, telling me about the barely-moving train, how it had latched onto her mother's fucking car stalled in the wrong fucking place, and pushed for way longer than a mile before the conductor could stop the engines, how her left leg was crumpled and shoved through a broken open hole in the floor of the new car, how the same leg sheered off below the knee by the ground rushing too fast and brutal, with blood flying, thrown paint, and Wendy asks one of the busboys for an order of rope, which he brings with a threatening air of impatience, and she's soon tying me up and making me listen to this. Like I said, I woke up fast even with the hangover.

I had a friend in college who enjoyed being tied up while making love, had a list of women who got off on it too—one of those things cocky and unfiltered egotistical men liked to reveal. I don't know what happened to the guy, but I wonder, now and again, if he's still alive, and this thought I place in that file marked *Morbid Curiosity*.

Roadway wanders into the bathroom and stretches out on the bath mat. Her operation was a success, but I have to feed her antibiotics for the next week. She growls when I get too close to the wound. I let Roadway have her space, and watch her go to sleep there, curling up like a shell. She tends to follow me into each room I visit in the house, and then leaves as another whim forces action—elliptical. When I step into the shower, the warm water soothes the pain of unrest. I close my eyes in the steam and feel the heat rising on my skin. I forget the dream and the slow-moving train.

I met Wendy at a fellow professor's party held in a modern home high up on the hillside above the inland cities, the tulip fields diamond-like in the farmland Spring distance towards the idyllic town of La Conner. Joseph and Anna dragged me to the shindig, coerced me into going with jovial kindheartedness. My only work friends, Joseph, and his wife, Anna, both taught at the college—Joe swirling in philosophy, and Anna stuck with cold statistics—they also lived on Fidalgo Island, and we sometimes carpooled if our schedules allowed it. Wendy was a friend of Anna's, but a better friend to Margo, my office mate, one of several other English Comp teachers all grouped together on campus in tiny offices. Wendy was someone new to the San Juan Island area who had been living here since last fall trying to start a fine arts gallery in Anacortes. I came from the area, and only left for the eight years it took me to get through college down state in Olympia, bum around with odd jobs before ducking back to graduate school in Portland, Oregon. I returned after those school years burned out by any fatuous promise of greatness.

Somehow, everyone in the English department thinks I inherited a lot of money, and it ain't all that much money in today's climate, but it's a house with a Puget Sound and Lopez Island view. After my father died while I was applying for grad school, everyone knew more than I did. Money caused more problems for me at the time because all I wanted to do was learn how to teach English well. I vowed never to go back to get my Ph.D. All of my grad school classmates acted like they knew the secret of my inner self, and how I'd make it one day, how I'd already made it, the un-American work ethic, the inheritance—your dad's a developer, and their voices perked up. No, he was only a realtor, and my town shut the conversation down. Then they'd ask if my mother was still living. How sad, they'd say, when I replied, "Barely." That being the only thing I could give before changing the subject. I would run from any further questions about my family. The most insouciant would later apologize for being too nosey about my personal life. There wasn't any reason to continue where we left off either. I was always departing.

At other times, pinned down, they'd ask me what I was going to do after graduation, a ceremony I wouldn't be attending. Another family emergency bloomed, my mother died a couple days before I would've walked up on stage to get a small piece of paper. She followed her mate, something common after long marriages. The patriarch expired, and finally, not too long after that, she'd passed away, and Jobeth told me I had to go to the funeral no matter how I felt. I told my pals I was going home, up north—to set up residency in my mother and father's old summerhouse. They told me how sorry they were—to be so young without any parents, but, when enough time passed, like a couple months, by telephone, on Facebook personal messages, they also added that they thought I was lucky; I'd be teaching in an area so pastoral, this formed by their city visions—too soaked in Portland's iconoclastic bustle.

Fidalgo Island is the Gateway to the San Juan Islands; it's where people catch the ferry to Lopez Island, Orcas, Friday Harbor or Victoria, British Columbia. I never tire of the Puget Sound view, the water mesmerizes me, and I will always fall for it.

Mount Vernon, where the community college campus is located, does have a Cascade mountain view visible from some of the luckier classroom windows. To get to work, it's a half hour drive to Mount Vernon, a fine, working-class town, divided by the Skagit River. Mount Vernon on one side, the city of Burlington on the river's other shore, where the big box stores and chain restaurants rule the boulevard: Costco, Best Buy, Olive Garden, and The Home Depot.

During the last two months of grad school, some of the less understanding started calling me Walden. They haven't seen the back end of Five Guys—the newest burger joint to hit the area, and far from Walden's imaginings.

"You're getting out of this goddamn city."

"You make sure we hear from you. Friend me on Facebook and share those killer pics of the island life on Instagram, dude."

What they were doing was making connections, schmoozing, trying to get something for nothing. I didn't feel lucky—my parents died. That was the cost of such luck. We make our own future. I believe in hard work. Money can't change that.

Again, my friends, Joseph and Anna, dragged me to the party. Joseph teaches philosophy with a wry smile always attached to any idea he wants to share. Sometimes, when I need to release the tension of the teaching track, I rally back and forth with him on the Anacortes public tennis courts— Anacortes is the name of the municipality on the island, named after Anna Curtis Bowman, but corrupted into Anacortes, allegedly due to illegible handwriting when the cursive on the official papers couldn't be read right. Joseph has a strong forehand and an inspiring kick serve. He usually wins every set unless he's stayed up too late the day before grading papers. I can get ahead of him if I keep the ball to his weaker backhand, and that's always a big if.

Joseph's wife, another Anna, very warm for a statistics genius, introduced me to Wendy, who stood next to Margo, looking pale and a bit skittish between the two women who wore black and blue bohemian shifts and turquoise bracelets as if they were long lost twins. I would've never thought Joseph and Anna liked to play matchmakers, but they knew the rules and followed through with easy wile. I remember Joseph asking me if I had met the woman in the corner talking to Anna and Margo. An open book up to this point, Joseph's dissembling grin ever present, alcohol-fueled, and making me think of lie-detector machines, I didn't think him the type to conceal his motivations; he never stopped tapping the rim of his wine glass until Wendy and I were making small talk about our respective pasts—she shielded her tendency to become a chatterbox, the grieving magpie persona was there though, ready to fly my way at the first sign of attention, caring, and even this thought, now, doesn't make me feel much guilt. Later that evening, once more separated, Anna asked Wendy, and Joseph asked me, if we were free for an informal dinner at their house in two days. We both accepted.

3

It's now weeks and weeks after that first
arranged dinner, and when I get to my office there's
an envelope taped to the door. On the outside of the
envelope is my first name written in spinster curls,
spidery frills. I walk inside and drop everything on
my bulky wooden desk. Margo is absent. I have the
office to myself. Margo only has meetings with her
students on Tuesdays and Thursdays. She rarely
uses her desk the other days since she lives on
Camano Island, the next town down the highway,
and quite a distance more to drive. I wonder if she
knows how I left Wendy alone at the restaurant,
whether they're close enough friends to have stayed
livid all weekend talking about how men have no
feelings.

The top of Margo's desk is pristine in its
tidiness. A large calendar desk blotter, a pen and
pencil holder, a tape dispenser and a box of tissue
make up the contents, and each item is spaced
evenly apart from the others. She owns and waters
the pale white orchid sitting on the window ledge,

and, on occasion, will ask me to water it if she knows she'll be away for too long. I told her not to hold me responsible if the plant dies. I have no luck with living plants; my house shows off the silk kind; they're placed on windowsills and table centerpieces; they're bought from catalogues with names like *Plant Art* or *Flower Couture,* and I never have to water them. Things are much simpler that way. With all the people I know in the flower business, including my sister, Jo, you'd think I'd be a convert to their ways. Jo can't stand the fake flowers and is always hiding them in storage closets, bringing me arrangements, when she visits. These die too quickly.

Margo's a startling woman. Whenever I see her I wonder why she isn't married, but I'll never ask her that—sounds so shallow—because we never have the inclination to carry on deep conversations: we're office mates. She diminishes her outer beauty with boxy clothes and heavy square glasses—she's screaming to be taken seriously. Again, I would never ask her why she chooses to do anything; I'm hardly a paragon of virtue, a role model, and I hide from the world most days, give only an outer shell of competence. I find myself rising to most pressing engagements with dread. She loves teaching English, and she doesn't complain about how today's students are as helpless as ever, robotic, perhaps, and dealing with low self-esteems, driven by a variety of societal forces. In fact, she doesn't say much of anything to me except hello, or how are you if we pass on campus, or if I happen to wander down here on Tuesdays. It's one of the attributes I like best about Margo. She keeps to herself.

The envelope is from a student of mine, and the note lets me know she can't make it to class today. Her name is Mrs. Claire Brown and she wants me to address her as Mrs. Brown. I told her to call me Professor Edwards. All the other students call me by my first name, Patrick, not Pat or Rick. Mrs. Brown is a nontraditional student, older than the others, older than me, and mother of two grade school children. She let it be known during the first few class sessions she said she waited to go back to school because of them—to be a role model. I didn't want to hear her reasons. She wanted to find someone to agree with her; to tell her she did the right thing by sacrificing her time, her youth, and that there's nothing wrong with being a mother and housewife.

I agree: there's not a thing wrong with staying out of the workforce and raising a family, but I gather from the piercing glances she continues to give me that she doesn't believe in my sincerity.

I tried to return to the lesson plan. She whispered to the other nontraditional student in the class and asked her why she was giving school another shot after so many years. The other woman, Marti Suber, told her it was none of her business, in a polite way, with a knowing chuckle. I passed out the next essay assignment, a practice outline, and the conversation pinged to something I could remain attached to: sentence structure, organization of paragraphs, and the essay on Nathaniel Hawthorne in the Life As Literature book.

As a teacher I sometimes wonder what the students think of what I do, and how well I do it. There is a wall between the teacher and the pupil; a distance I keep by building seriousness into each daily lesson. Mrs. Claire Brown shows me her resentment with every word she speaks in class and every facial expression—she makes me think of my mother for one second each time I see her—and I conceal my unsettled dread most of the time. If I talked to my colleagues more, down at the union cafeteria, Mrs. Brown would be a humorous topic of conversation, which would spur the other teachers to talk about their students, and how there's always one in every class who gives you the chills. I don't think I could listen to them talk about their Mrs. Claire Browns.

The office telephone rings. It sits on the small table between Margo's desk and my own. I feel put upon simply having to stand and move over to the chirping thing, to answer it—such an old feeling shivers its way into my mind—I am too used to answering an iPhone. I slouch in the extra office chair and say hello into the receiver. The shouting bursts forth and the phone bobbles in my grasp. The words spew forth, angry and seething, puncture something within my psyche, and I wince.

"You'll get yours, *Teacher*." The cadence of the words plays manic and spit-fresh quick. "You're no longer at an unreachable distance—Fucker."

Then, immediate silence, a dead tone fills the line as I glance out the open office door to see if someone has possibly heard, which is absurd—the scream was so loud I actually thought that. I collect myself, run a hand across my face and pretend nothing out of the ordinary has happened. Wendy's image floats in front of me: her sagging mouth and the words she spoke last Friday night about death and what it really means. The voice on the line wasn't hers. I'm quite sure of it. Her voice is soft and timid, exploring, an earnest yearning for every mystery to be explained. Then again it could've been Wendy camouflaging her voice in rage, somehow distorting what was so bitter the past date night, showing me how it feels to leave someone in a vulnerable lurch.

The voice repeats itself over and over again. I hear it in my mind. I try to decipher it. Who it was? What it means: *unreachable distance—Fucker*.

I call Joseph's office and let it ring six times before hanging up. I would've asked him what to do. You bet I'd let Joseph listen to my latest problem: *Joseph . . . it's me. How's Anna? No, Wendy and I aren't doing all that great. I'm okay.*

Listen, Joseph, I just got a strange telephone call. Didn't think people still made prank calls. It's one of those old campus phones with no caller ID. I don't know who it was. Maybe an angry student? The voice sounded muffled, like a woman's. Whoever it was sure is angry with me. It could've been a student. She said, you'll get yours, Teacher. You're no longer unreachable, no, wait, that's not right, she said, exactly, at an unreachable distance, and hung up after adding Fucker to the message. You really think so? I'll try not to worry about it then. Kids play all sorts of games. Thanks for your time, Joseph. See you soon. Then again, I don't think talking to Joseph is such a good thing right now. He'd ask me a lot of questions about Wendy and I'd feel compelled to tell Joseph I didn't want to talk about it. Joseph wouldn't want to hear that all his hard work bringing two eligible people together was for nothing, and I don't want to hear him, the philosophy professor turned controlling matchmaker, lecture me for minutes on what I did wrong, philosophically.

The day passes with sameness, repeated waves slapping a beach. So many similar problems to address: students who forgot to write their papers over the weekend (um, not putting up with that at all and make a check by their names in my gradebook), students who need next week's assignments because they're going on family vacations, students who come into class late, saunter to the back row and stare at me as if I were the deciding member of their parole board. I want to shake them sometimes. I swear, sometimes I do. I wonder if I could pay Mrs. Claire Brown to do it for me. I could take her into my confidence and make her my star pupil, stop her from giving me the evil eye. I could redirect her anger away from me and put it to good sycophantic use. The college would give her a citation for stirring interest in the student body, for making them sit up and take notice for once.

On the ride home I feel empty. The emptiness comes from guilt. Wendy's been on my mind since my solitary dinner at the College Café, where a buffet of chopped iceberg lettuce, five-bean salad, taco meat and stale tortillas filled the two serving carts. If Wendy had eaten with me tonight I would've listened to her, intently, so seriously that

I'd be able to recite our conversation from memory forty years from now.

If I live that long, I'd listen to her mother's story, how it's shaping her present mindset, and I'd ask if she had any other relatives: father, brothers, sisters, grandparents, or cousins to speak of. I'd ask her how often she dreams about trains and the sound of the whistle blowing from afar, warning of the impending turn around the corner. As it steams through the towns, does your dead mother haunt you in your dreams? Do you tell her not to drive across the tracks where her car will stall? Does she ignore you, Wendy? Does she smile at you before the train hits? Are her teeth tombstones? Is this all there is? I cross the train tracks every time I drive to work, and sometimes, when stopped by the short freighters, waiting for the crossbar to rise, I see blood.

On the way home, I imagine the lights across The Sound distanced by time, an age separating the town of Anacortes. It's as if the place hasn't changed in over a hundred years. I drive down the road as if I'm heading to the Ferry Terminal and then take a left, drive up to a ridge with an expansive view twinkling between trees, and park in front of my cottage, my parents' summer cottage. The water makes a slithery snake sound against the rocks far below me, and I think about the last time laughter filled the house, Victorian, of an older epoch, when boisterous siblings played games, a family unit ruled the rafters—later, mice and ants abandoning the rafters, too chilled by the interior atmosphere.

The first thing I do after I unlock my door and flick on the hall light is pick up the kitchen telephone and call Wendy. I let it ring and ring five times before I hear the click of someone picking the receiver up. It's Wendy, it has to be Wendy because she lives alone, and she says, "Hello?"

"Wendy? It's me." And there's nothing more I can say. My tongue refuses to move. It sticks to the bottom of my mouth.

"This isn't Wendy, but I know who you are. You leave her alone. Haven't you caused enough damage?" The stranger hangs up. My thoughts race in my mind trying to figure out who spoke to me: Margo? Anna? Then, I dwell on what to do next, if anything, why I even tried in the first place, and I wonder how many other people know about what I did.

Roadway, muck-brown and white fur ridged with irritation, limps over to where I'm standing and growls softly. Her tail is bent to the left, the tip twitching. I pick her up as gently as possible and take her over to the food dish. Roadway's belly is still ripe. Raw red lines meet together to form an X on her stomach. Because of the sutures, black and wiry, the scars look like train tracks colliding, forming something unspeakably painful.

4

I can't go to sleep. I stay up all night grading
essays because I need something to do. I move to
the easy chair facing the Sound—the outlines of the
islands in the distance another darkness. Roadway
yawns and moans like an asthmatic when I jostle
my feet too much. Usually when I read student
writing I have no trouble falling asleep. The
fractured sentences and passive verbs lull me into
slumber. This time I keep thinking about the date I
ruined. I can't believe I actually abandoned Wendy,
but I know I'd do it again. As I hold my blue pen
and make checks next to the ungrammatical
sentences, Roadway sleeps, shuddering and
shaking on the ottoman, and I want to join her in
slumber so that I can defend her from whatever
makes her body contort. This is not the way I'm
supposed to live. I didn't do anything so terribly
wrong to Wendy. We just didn't hit it off. Okay,
leaving someone in the middle of a restaurant is
pretty low, especially after she'd cut herself open
and divulged her pain for me and anyone within

earshot to witness, and I want to apologize. Next time I see her, I will, and take what's coming to me.

The first month Wendy and I saw each other was a happy fluke. I do have pleasant memories of the few times, twice, we walked together across campus after Wendy decided to surprise me in my office, just showed up.

"I'm shopping at Costco. Do you need a big block of Gruyere? Does Margo need anything?" I'd think: I don't know. How could I know?

"Please ask Margo when she comes back." My inner answer forming: Call her on your cell. You're better friends with her. You know she only comes to her office on Tuesdays and Thursdays. I just said, "Sure."

Wendy had a habit of asking questions I had no idea of what the answer could possibly be. Things changed when she got too serious, when this following, needy behavior began—I didn't want Wendy to become a barnacle. Nowadays I want to take my social life a bit slower, less entwined with romantic maneuvers. Months of dating could go by before I'd ask anyone new in my life about her family and when I could meet them for a backyard barbecue. With Wendy, and a handful of others, she felt quickly compelled to catch me up on her family history.

Am I so different from anyone else? I can't be the only one in the world who likes to take his time, who is wary of commitments, the only person who is worried about STDs, scandals, and inappropriate public displays of affection. I've heard a statistician say that one out of six men who reach their forties without ever being married will actually go through with a wedding. What happens to the other five single men? Are they treated like pariahs? Will I be one of the five? Because I'm in my early thirties, and I've never walked down the aisle, I get it that people think I'm strange in some way, lacking something. Some people believe I'm a closeted homosexual, and that's okay too; gets me off the hook. I can roll with that. On Fidalgo Island, rumors abound. I've never let this bother me before.

The people who fear differences are the ones that structure the rules. I play by these rules. Gays and lesbians can get married—I've never ever wanted to get close to marriage—and some righteous people still think they're all sodomites and spreaders of infection, and not worthy to enter the institution, mate for life. What do gay people do that straight people don't—who am I to judge when so many have turned around and judged me? Sex shouldn't be an issue. I know of too many hetero men who brag about the different positions they and their partners have had sex in—I think of the guy from college with the S/M fetish, who carried an overnight bag filled with different ropes and scarves, something I found a bit creepy to carry around in his car. Do gay people date any differently in the age of AIDS? Eric, my friend from grad school, still lives in Chicago. After our first year as students in the English program, when I was starting to get to know him, he told me how lonely he was; that there wasn't anyone in the city who wanted a lasting relationship, and how scared he was of becoming HIV positive, teenage years in the age of managed care, marginalization; really more scared of being tested, which just made me mad inside if he wasn't being safe in the first place.

"Gotta do it, man." I told him I wished more people were concerned about the disease (it's now an invisible illness no one talks about much anymore since drugs prolong the lives of those who have it—young people today being short-sighted and thinking there's a pill for it so why play safe?), people still feared talking about it much—as if in a chase with real-life cooties, but in the back of my mind I wondered if he was about to proposition me (I can't help being boorish at times—I'm not that freakin' attractive, but I've seen this pattern before with both men and women who I allow to get this close to me—at some point, the friendship turns to yearning, a bright shiny earnestness: look at me in a different way) so I clammed up and finally told him to keep trying to find the right mate, risk it, or change cities.

He said, "I know what you're thinking. Thanks for being a smartass. You're not my type." We parted. We went to our offices. No one knows what I'm thinking.

It was another classmate, Cheryl, who informed me Eric was gay. Cheryl relished her role as the gossip of the department. She thought she was being nonchalant, hip, the queen of open mindedness, when she told me this, and then said she didn't care one way or another if he was gay because Eric was a great guy. She said her mother had told her that a gay man could be one of the closest friends a straight woman could ever have because there isn't the usual sexual tension or game playing. I told Cheryl I must get to an appointment and left her there, sitting on the administration steps ready to eat her untoasted bagel. Later, I heard, from Eric, that Cheryl told him and a few other grad students I was still in the closet, and hadn't come to terms with my sexuality—even used that old cliché *denial is a river in Egypt.* At first I was angry, not about the gay part, but about the idle gossip, small minds; Eric calmed me down and told me no one who knew me believed her.

"Let her get her kicks," Eric said. "Everyone thinks she's just bitter because you didn't show any interest in her."

"I just don't want to get involved right now, with anybody," I said.

"I wish I didn't want to," Eric replied, "but you're probably safer playing the celibate. You can't trust anyone's sexual history these days—*these days* meaning: because of his overblown fear of contracting a disease and dying.

The last time Eric called to ask me how I was, I told him all about the job, the generic students, the weather, and Roadway. He really listened to me. I didn't have any major problems; I was happy. I remember listening to him with one ear as I read the local paper online, surfed the internet news of the moment, wrote some tweets on Twitter, and heard him talk about a man he had just broken up with.

"I just can't date anyone for more than two months; things start to go wrong. I start to get too attached."

I supplied the, 'Uh-huhs . . .' and the occasional 'That's too bad' at the right time, and he continued his monologue style of conversing, something Eric was good at. I called it filibustering. At the end of our conversation he told me he always had a spare bedroom waiting for me when I came to town, and his last words were, "Get out more. Stop being so old fashioned. I bet there are a lot of unattached women dying to find someone as honest and as open as you are." If Eric truly believes that I'm an open person, a book anyone can read, he doesn't know me that well, and this is the persona I revealed to him, only one surface, one reflection from life's mirror, and he seldom ever tried to dig deeper—as I prefer.

I can picture these unattached women. They are distorted, their features sharper, yet magnified to enhance certain characteristics. Wendy is the first in an endless line. She stands in front of me with her arms coalescing into one arm, forming a circle. This circle wraps over my head until it pulls me forward, putting pressure on my back. The circle-arm pushes me close until Wendy and I are pressed together. Her eyes become mirrors, and I look into them and see my mother behind me, her reflection looming on my living room wall like a shade from the past. I cry out—I am not the kind of guy who speaks out loud to himself—and the illusion fades.

5

On Tuesday, when I arrive at my office after lunch, the gift-wrapped present rests on my desk. My office mate, Margo, sits with her head bent down. Silent, she's flipping through papers, marking grades in her leather-bound ledger. I say hello and she looks up, smiles, and says hello back to me.

"How're you doing? Looks like you were up late grading papers. I was too." I realize what my words mean, and say, "Not that you look bad, just like you didn't get much sleep. You have a lot of papers." My words don't mean anything anymore.

"No offense taken, Patrick. You, on the other hand, look like shit. Did you pull an all-nighter?"

I laugh. Can't help it. Margo is funny. The purple rings under my eyes are puffy; even a long shower couldn't revive my sluggish toxic wasted state.

Margo continues with her papers. Her manner unchanged towards me, unmodified, she's still friendly, has always been friendly to me, and I wonder if she's spoken with Wendy.

I lay my briefcase beside the box on my desk and stare at the writing. Only my first name is written across the top using a dull silver Sharpie, the box wrapped with tight corners of lilac paper. A gift?

"Margo? Did you notice who put this on my desk?"

"I didn't see anyone this morning, but I did yesterday afternoon when I dropped in to get some aspirin and to work on my own writing. A nontraditional student of yours dragged her screaming child up and down the hallway. She spent fifteen minutes reading all the notices for poetry and fiction gatherings on the bulletin board. Stayed quite a long time even after I told her you weren't around." Margo opened her laptop, kept on doing what she needed to get done.

"Thanks, Margo. I must've just missed you, and I'm happy to've missed that student. I know who you're talking about. At least she doesn't bring her kid to class."

"Set my migraine into overdrive." Margo said this as if she was blaming me. I couldn't read her well. She reminded me of my sister who loved to tease me.

"Sorry to hear."

"Anyway, the box was outside the office door when I came in. You have an admirer. Pretty paper." Margo clears her throat and once again concentrates on her work. I can't help feeling like a teenager again, Jo irritating me to no end about girlfriends and sex. I remember Wendy coming to visit Margo last week, before the trouble at dinner, and how happy they looked, Wendy disturbed by the amount of work a new gallery needs, but happy nonetheless. Was the package from Wendy?

The wrapping gives way and a tiny white box, the size of a paperback book, is revealed. When I take the top off the box I see the tiny doll cradled in purple tissue. My black hair is cut short, conservative, with a part on the right side. So is the doll's hair, and it looks as if it's woven from fine strands of my own hair. My brown eyes are large and the left eye is a little bit lower than the right. So are the doll's eyes: uneven. It looks like me, and when I take the doll out I see the hatpin, long and sleek with a pearl capping one end, skewered through the doll's head, from ear to ear.

Before I can contain myself, before my own heart can stop its rise in beats, Margo jolts me away from my thoughts by saying, "It looks like whoever sent you *that* is a different type of admirer." My breath catches and I sit down with the doll in my left hand in front of me.

"Who would send such a thing?" I want to demand the truth out of Margo instead—only because she's here. She knows. I know she knows, but that's only an assumption. She's lying. I don't know if she's lying. And I press my bewilderment away.

"I haven't a clue. Someone sick. I back away from the crazy, and I get a lot of them, students, an ex-husband who would get off on doing something like this, but you don't have an ex-husband." She holds her hands up, palms out to placate my next thought, and says, "Kidding. Sorry. Do you want me to call security? I think you should report it. Get it on record." I don't know what to think. A list of people who know me intimately runs through my head. It's a very short list. Since I moved back to the area permanently, I've dated two women. Jackie Beamer, a florist (am I drawn to women who act like my sister? Have the same interests? Another question to ask any future therapist) who turned fashion designer, came first, and then Suzanne Parminter, a chiropractor. Two women with strong identities, both pursued their own careers with tenacious charisma, and held down jobs in the same town.

Jackie and I went out for four months, probably a record for me. She didn't want a commitment, and neither did I. We were happy with the small engagements, pressureless, going to the movies together with no attachments. She thought she broke my heart when she told me she was moving to California to start up a clothing design company with a friend, a rich friend, following her dream; she said her floral business was in the gutter—a barbed comment. No one bought flowers outside of major holidays anymore—the obligatory political comment attached: in this current climate . . . I didn't let her know she wasn't breaking my heart. Jackie irked me with her continuous doom and gloom outlook on flowers; she knew my sister ran a thriving floral and gifts operation closer to Seattle. I couldn't bring up Jo's business in her presence. I remembered my hubris in even offering to ask Jo if she'd meet Jackie, give her some helpful tips. Wouldn't have worked out. That proffered meeting . . . or, Jackie and I.

About a month after Jackie closed shop and skipped town, I met Suzanne Parminter in one of the two local Starbucks while reading the morning paper and eating breakfast croissants with microwaved ham. She asked what the headline was and could she borrow the Business section. I shared my paper and found myself telling her about a seminar on foreign trade being held the following week at the city center, that another rally cry was going out to all citizens—it sounded just boring enough, and I didn't actually think she'd want to accompany me. We both ended up going, sitting next to each other, and eating dinner afterwards at Adrift. She knew almost nothing about me, and nothing about my new teaching position. Suzanne, a local chiropractor, only talked about two things, and when she wasn't talking about children, future children, family, she talked about her financial situation; caught up in the current post-economic collapse, a countrywide shellacking, a correction in the housing market—see how great this economy is doing under my leadership—that helped only those millionaires, billionaires, with disposable incomes, the slyest of lies now the new norm. The last looming, double-dipper, financial disaster worries made her more than anxious, and years later , after digging out of the stressful trenches, I believed her every future decision rested on what the Greeks did. Who's really better off today than they were eight years ago? I wouldn't hold up my hand. I wanted to tease her, tell her that I was going to the top of Mt. Erie, the highest point on Fidalgo Island, to consult with The Oracle of Anacortes, get the scoop.

We dated but never got serious. She wanted children too damn much, and I could see this covetous glint invade every single time a mother pushing a stroller entered the Starbucks; she kept bringing them up in conversation. Do you like girls or boys? If you had to choose, right now, would you want a girl or a boy? I want any child of mine to have a sound economic future, don't you? And I'd smile and nod. Suzanne would continue her harangue on the state of the mess we're all in. Now she's married to someone she met holding a peace placard at the local Sunday protest movement, blue vs. red, rich vs. poor, stupid vs. smart, those with gold stars on their bellies vs. those without stars on their bellies, who gather on the four opposing corners of Commercial Avenue right outside the Anacortes Safeway—during an election year the amount of people there sometimes gets crazy small town wild with maybe 20 protesters on each side of whatever issue squawking back and forth. I never make eye contact with any of them, and never choose a side.

When I cross paths with Suzanne doing island errands, I always listen to her small talk. I've never believed in chiropractic theory, but we drink the occasional cup of coffee together in the mornings before work, and I seldom bring up her job.

Last week, she said, "Patrick, one day you'll open up to me, or to someone else, and you'll realize that you don't have anything to hide. You're not unreachable; there's a girl out there who's perfect for you." Then she told me she was two months pregnant and isn't it great? She's not hiding anything anymore. I couldn't give her what she coveted.

Jackie or Suzanne . . . it can't be either of them.

The phone call? The voodoo doll? Jackie, Suzanne, Wendy. The three women I dated since moving back to Fidalgo Island for good.

Margo talks to security. She hangs up and tells me that someone is on the way. She says, "I hope you find out who sent it. I've got to go teach my class. See you later. Let me know what happens." I don't keep in touch socially with Margo. This is a first, and what strangeness.

She leaves and I'm left with the voodoo doll.

I take the wrapping paper with the spidery handwriting and go over to Margo's desk. There're a few curling Post-It notes attached in a row, three pink ones, and I compare her blocky cursive with the doll-sender's script, and realize Margo couldn't have written the note, but I'm not an expert in handwriting—the capacity for good people to be manipulative, secretive, dangerously mad, at times, is well known to me. My mother's icy parenting as primer. Jo tells me she never wants to hear me trash our mom again. Don't speak ill of the dead. Around her, I resist the instant urge, but nowhere else. When drunk, more and more, I can't keep her image (I insert fangs, devil horns) from making me feel worse. I'd blame my mother for this doll prank if she were still drawing each foul breath. Now, though, an unknown third party is involved: Me, whoever sent the doll, probably the same injured and angered troll who made the prank call, and Margo. The campus security guard, a fourth party, is on the way. He'll ask me things about my personal life and I'll have to tell him more than I'm comfortable with, keep details sketchy, as I always do, and look like an uncooperative fool. They'll say: *You called us, Buddy.*

6

***

My sister's coming over tonight and for once
I don't mind her company. Jo arrives at six to take
me to dinner. Actually, I'm taking her to dinner to
cheer her up—it wasn't too long ago her husband,
Steve, a boob of a lost soul, found a flashy, red-
haired, fiery Costco executive from Kirkland to fall
in love with, the cad telling Jo his adulterous
confession a couple days before what would've been
their 8th anniversary—but we're going in her car.
She's driving her old sky-blue, beat-up, four-door
Mercedes sedan with 190,000 miles tacked on it.
It's painted with her flower shop logo: A Burst of
Spring, a bunch of sixties-style daisies on the hood
and rear door panels. I want to ask her how the
floral business is thriving in this worrisome climate
(after the last election, locally, and there were more
than a few students dropping out altogether to join
the low-paying workforce; customers weren't
calling as much, squirrels storing up nuts for the
long winter haul), have her compare whines with

Jackie's past comments. But, I'm wrong, and my sister isn't treading water. She says she's having the time of her life—filling up her free moments away from Steve—at least they didn't have kids. Like me, Jo says she doesn't want them either. We are two peas in a pod on that issue. She's breathless with expansion ideas, branching out with a Gifts and Coffee Pot Café in the space next to her floral shop—it's what you have to do. The old car was a long-ago gift from Steve in better, early times, but rather than trade it in for a newer model Jo thought she could advertise better with a stylized Mercedes. I'm thinking about the afternoon and how the security guard, a woman named Lorraine—not the *he* I, being sexist, apology, assumed would show up—took my statement with an impatient and snobbish tone. She more or less dismissed the doll and the telephone call. She told me to forget about it. It's probably someone you failed. Any of them hanging around just call me again?

"It's simply a harmless prank. Students here do some crazy shit." I heard: *Indubitably, it's elementary, my dear, the children of today can get up to such mischief!* She said she'd file a report—

when she got around to it later in the afternoon. I was outraged, but I didn't show or tell Lorraine that. I kept my frustration hidden inside. "It's not such a big deal anyway . . . probably part of a campus dare," Lorraine said. "I've seen stranger shit go down here than a hoodoo doll, believe me." She said this to reassure me.

Jobeth waltzes into my house, moves as if she still owns part of every nook; this was her house too when we were kids. She acts like she'll always be part owner, that it's her house forevermore. Then again, she behaved that way when Mother and Father were alive. Every time she comes over she makes an inventory list in her mind as she scans every piece of furniture and china, or the paintings lining the upper hall. The house is decorated in late seventies era sailor, a man's ship, with father's insistence on mirrors on the side walls to reflect the sunset, make the living room appear larger than it is. My mother went along with this but hung photos and paintings everywhere else. Most of the time I'm sitting and looking at my own reflection, watching Roadway scamper up the stairs to what were our childhood bedrooms, three of them small enough to fit a twin bed, a dresser, a lot of pop posters, and little more. After our mother died we divided everything. Jobeth took all that she wanted, which was quite a bit more than what she left. I didn't mind, and I still don't. She walks in and says hello to me while she opens the buffet drawer and takes out grandmother's antique silver asparagus server. The dark heavy oak furniture, dining table, chairs, gathers dust.

"I forgot about this, Patrick. I've been thinking about it for a month now. The last dinner Steve served before we separated was an elaborate plea for reconciliation. I could've used this." She fiddles with the silver handle and I tell her she can have it. I don't eat asparagus anyway. A lie to smooth over my irritation; arguing against Jo's claim to every little memento from the past would bring nothing but more insufferable conversation.

"You should, Patrick, and broccolini, and bananas, turmeric, blueberries, and, oh, as many sweet potatoes you can manage—put cinnamon in your morning coffee." She adds more organic produce to her list as I listen. I see each word as a picture the instant she says it, glistening pomegranate seeds, pumpkin mash, lemongrass, ginger, and instead of ground beef, switch it out for bison.

"We really should be going. I'm starved. Aren't you?" My simple statement deflates her most-nutritious-foods-to-eat monologue, and she tightens her mouth, her upper lip a thin line, peeved, like our mother's. She takes a deep breath, touches up her hair in the wall mirror. I can imagine her counting to ten, not wanting our dinner to begin badly.

"Sure. Starved." Jobeth puts the silver asparagus tongs in her purse, but it's too long and the flat head protrudes. She is sad: her blonde hair is damp as if she didn't have time to dry it after her shower, and she looks beaten. I haven't talked to her since she hung up on me. This dinner was her idea, but I know she must think I'm immature for playing games with her. I tell her I have all the time in the world to listen to her and that I care about her.

She comes over and puts her arms around me as if my plea to get to the restaurant and return home quick (this part an assumption only) is forgiven. I hug her back, not too hard, the usual, and the asparagus server digs into my side. I think of my vision, a weak moment, arms conjoining, circling. We cling to each other and then part like two acquaintances meeting after a long time, both wondering if they showed too much awkward emotion instead of giving air-kisses. We are siblings, related by blood, unresponsive Uncles and Aunts on both sides due to a rift a long generation ago, and I wish I'd learned who caused this estrangement. We don't know our cousins, and these number in the dozens, the invites to each family reunion unopened.

At Dos Amigos, the *Immediate Seating* sign brilliant red, the only decent, festive pseudo-Mexican restaurant on the island, I tell Jo I hope the karaoke music filtering in from the bar area, umbrellas in the margaritas, chips and salsa, cheery waitresses, silent but happy busboys, will make us both feel better. I know neither of us will be getting up on the small stage to mangle any tune from the past fifty years. I sit there smiling at my sister. It's not my all-power smile, the one I use when I greet my class on the very first day of the school term; it's my smile to let Jo know I'm relating to her like the brother I am; that secret smile we used as children when we stared at each other across the dinner table, Father, a proper pillar of the community, to the left of me, Mother, a rigid presence, on my right. I barely made eye contact with any of them, can't even remember the color of my father's eyes at the moment, blue, green, a mixture of both, and this fact startles me. I find myself smiling but stricken by the past and its disturbing moments. Why are these always the first to resurface?

Jo says, "Why are you so damn happy? You look strange."

"I was just thinking about all the family dinners, countless Sunday roasts, baby corn, and sweet potato pie from Alanson's Bakery."

"Remember the time we took the yam pie up to Cap Sante viewpoint and ate the entire thing one afternoon? All the hell we took when we confessed," Jo says, her voice tinged with dormant longing, as if she'd go back in an instant if offered the chance, still incapable of realizing that the moments in our shared past, the good not outweighing the bad, should stay in the past. Regret is the bitterest pill, and I extinguish this thought the next moment, become agreeable, the agreeable child, once more.

"You say yam. I say sweet potato. I know. I know. You don't need to tell me again. I should eat one every single day." I chuckle, a little two-beat laugh. "I remember the happy times." I say this while the waitress sets a bowl of tortilla chips and two salsas on the table. She says the red kind is fiery hot and the green kind is without jalapeños, only flavorful green chilies—the seeds in the milder one make it look spicier. She takes our margarita order and twirls away. No salt for Jo.

"So." I taste sandpaper in my throat and tension (is an apparition keeping us company) filters in, but I plow on. "The last few weeks must've been rough for you. I'm very sorry." There's nothing more I can bring myself to say. I try to concentrate on her reaction, every twitch of her cheekbones, and each upward point of an eyebrow. She's keeping everything in control and she reminds me of our mother so much when I look at her. The voice in my head begs me to get up and run again, quick and far.

Jo tilts her head to the left and bites into a chip. She then takes a gulp of water and tells me I'll really like the red salsa. "You've always loved spicy things. I couldn't stand them, but I did read that eating red chilies helps extend life by up to thirteen per cent. Isn't that incredible?" Now I want to tell her to stick to the green salsa—the shortened lifespan diet has some macabre appeal. "I've been depressed for a long time now and I want you to know that you didn't help me. I used to think I could count on you. My big brother." She's trying her best to make me feel guilty, and it's beginning to work. I wonder how many times I'll have to say I'm sorry, and if she'll even hear me if I did.

"I said I was sorry. Listen, I'm here now." The large party of people next to us, sitting along the banquet tables, chants happy birthday to a teenager named Buddy in a staccato burst. It's common in these parts to have nicknames, and this is a big fishing and sailing community, where all the boat hands are sent to Western or the University of Washington; they come back in the summer to drink, sail, run around in their fathers' cars, spend money like thieves, and act like they're bored by breathing. The question I'm often asked by other locals I'm supposed to know, is: Oh, where do you spend the dreary, rainy, gothic winter? Jennie and I head to Oaxaca before the first Pacific Nor'easter makes landfall. Because I have a recognizable Island name, and a past, no one forgets an ill-favored moment from history, two parents these locals thought had both too much free time and an imaginary amount of money, gold, stocks, glittery riches, I'm included in their peripheral retirement planning. Every June I'm invited to the pre-solstice party by someone who remembers my parents, and the smiling woman from the Yacht Tree Arts Council always comes around to ask me for another donation. My parents were frugal, but they spent the bulk of their wealth over the decade since my father bought, and then quickly sold, his boat—took lavish vacations to Zihuatanejo and became unapologetic boozehounds during their month-long sojourn every February. By the time they arrived back home, I hardly recognized them. For the weeks we couldn't join them as kids and then teenagers—our schooling came first, and don't look so glum, mommy and daddy need some time away, alone together, to heal, you'll join us during your spring break—a nanny would look after us, a chaperone, and these women's names I'll not soon forget: Alice, Patty, a barnacle of a spinster named Kristina Perkins took her job too seriously, whipped us with her malicious mindset, and our parents loved her best. They paid her well to keep Jo and I in line during the high school years, when our parents chose to abdicate their familial duties even more. I could escape to Zihuatanejo today, sit under a thatched umbrella, eat fresh caught fish tacos daily, watch Canadians walk back and forth across the crescent beach, drink Basil Crushes—follow in my father's footsteps.

"Mother would say things like that to us. Remember? I don't think she cared one whit about us after father died," Jo says, a hook in her throat.

I can't respond to that now. They were together, married so many years, but died young, both almost reaching the age of 65, never enjoyed an extended silver-lining retirement, and I don't ever think about my own retirement age—why save for something so ethereal? Mother's image claws its way in and my breathing becomes irregular. I want to change the subject. The waitress comes back and asks me if I'm Patrick.

"Yes." I rub my fingers on my paper napkin.

She hands me a plain white envelope with *Please give to Patrick customer* written on the flap in familiar spidery lines. My eyes betray myself to Jo. I don't want to open it. The waitress stays in anticipation. Jobeth says, "Curious, Patrick," and then she giggles like there are better days ahead.

"Who gave you this?" The waitress shrugs.

"It was on front counter. I saw nobody."

> To the waitress, I say, "We'll be ready to order in a minute." She takes the cue and leaves.

"Who's it from?"

"If I knew that I wouldn't be so mystified." I rip open the envelope and tug out a small piece of yellow-lined notepaper. Written on the paper are the words: *A bomb will explode ten minutes after you read this—You Bastard! You and your new girlfriend better get out. YOU caused this!!!!!!*

I can't speak. My face drains of color because Jobeth asks me what's wrong and then yanks the paper out of my hand.

"We've got to get out of here." She stands and grabs her purse, the color draining from her face. "We have to tell the manager, call the police. Who does things like this? In this day and age?" She's more than upset, immediately frantic, and talking in a continuous stream, almost yelling. I'm not listening. I'm thinking of bombs going off—the senseless destruction, loss of lives, and the physically and emotionally wounded. I'm thinking about who wrote the note, who sent me the doll, the crazy woman following me around town watching my every move. My sister grabs me by the hand, pulling, and we stop at the hostess stand, we're making quite a scene already. The manager leans on the wooden platform and contemplates where he should seat an elderly couple. Jo clamps a hand onto his arm and takes him aside; the elderly couple huff and frown. My sister hands him the paper and says a waitress just gave the note to me. She points at me. His face turns red. No time to dance the Bamba.

* * *

Pressure builds inside and then all around me. It's there, firing like a steam engine, cornering my responsibilities into strands of bitter guilt. I sit in an uncomfortable straight-back metal folding chair and stare at Jobeth out of the corner of my left eye. Across from both of us sits a policeman, a detective named Waters, and another plainclothes underling. We've been in this room for hours. The letter, the note with my first name on the outside is in a plastic bag, and Waters handles it with a grace reserved for taxidermists. This will make the national radar after the Seattle news stations speak about a tense situation close to their shores—and then they'll bring up old images of other dreadful acts. This time, thankfully, it's only a false alarm.

Police, the men and women of the Anacortes Fire Department, aided by the Washington State Patrol Explosives Unit, roared into life a minute after the manager called. By then, most of the diners in the restaurant stood corralled outside and far from the restaurant. They couldn't even collect their cars until the next day. Those who had finished eating ate for free; the rest were given coupons for a complimentary meal. I don't see how any of them would return after a bomb scare. I won't be dining there again, but then, the manager doesn't want me to come back. It was in his eyes as the place deserted on a busy Tuesday night. They locked onto mine and I could feel the blame rushing, pricking into me, and I tried to shield myself by bowing my head and following Jobeth.

It was just a scare. There was no bomb, but might as well have been for all the bad press it will cause. The local paper wants to interview me now. I decline, the first of many, but a lot of other people will talk. They'll say they witnessed the whole thing: how a spindly Ichabod Crane of a man and a blonde woman who looked like him caused a lot of commotion at the local Mexican fiesta palace. I'm beginning to wish Jo and I had simply left without saying anything. But then, what if this imaginary bomb hadn't been so imaginary?

"Do you have any idea, any idea at all, why someone would want to play this kind of trick?" Detective Waters asks us. He includes Jobeth in his question, but expects me to answer. I'm beginning to feel like a criminal, someone with something to hide—and then I explain everything about the prank phone call and the voodoo doll.

7

Before she leaves to drive back home to
Seattle the next morning, Jo says she'll move in for
a while if I want her to. I tell her I'll call if I need
company and give her a tight hug goodbye. We look
into each other's eyes and I feel like a real brother,
someone relating to another person through an
unbreakable bond. I don't want Jo to leave.

I'm supposed to go on an unplanned vacation.
The police told me to stop working for a week, to
stay at home and see if things settle down. Bomb
scares are nothing to scoff at, Waters said. Someone
out there wants to hurt you. We take these
occurrences with the utmost responsibility.

I told them all about my past: Wendy's name
kept coming up, and I felt guilty. I see her face
again as I wander around my house, the same place
I raced through as a child, with Jo following and
teasing me—out of sight and not to be heard. How
did we ever grow up? Is it like this for everyone? Do
they feel the loss of youth as much as I do? Years
pass like a movie not good enough to stay awake

for, nodding off and then becoming alert towards the end, which isn't earned: one day you're young, guileless, ordered and ruled in straight by those who raise you, and the next day, after a long night filled with dreams, nightmares, you wake up, safe, alone, an adult out in the world, and everything else is a memory, distant in its specificity. I remember my father, and I feel no lingering hatred; he did the best he could. He's pictured in a frame on the stair landing, strong in a darker-than-night navy suit, off to church or a wedding (or, the funeral), or work in the real estate office downtown—really just an excuse to be seen as a man of the people, even though my father had no political ambitions. He appears crushed by time, and the yellowing of the photograph by the sunlight day after day is an honorable badge. My mother is nowhere in this house anymore. Her photos won't haunt me again except in my dreams where she came when I was young to splinter me down like kindling and throw me into the fire.

Evening comes quicker than I expected as time loops even more when I'm caught in the backdraft of such nastiness aimed in my direction. A half day after Jo departed with her tight frown the morning after the *incident*; that's how she's referring to it now—she reminded me so much of our mother at that moment—the telephone rings. I actually answer it but there's no one on the line and I hang up. I feel lost. I believe the person calling is someone who wants to do me harm, and by picking up the receiver I've just told that person I am home. I welcome that person. Come on over, throw me off the cliff right into the Sound, if that's your dark wish.

I live on an island, where 100-year-old-and-older cottages were built and handed down to family, generation to generation. My home is part of a private association, but not gated. Out of the six homes that make up our little bluff outcropping, only three other families live here year round; the rest are summer and winter snowbirds with big RVs, those retirees who can afford to keep a second vacation home. Most are old sprawling Victorian beach cottages, and even with today's rising property taxes, I'm happy I only have one tax bill due. I feel pushed in during the summer, when all the island cottages and homes fill up with children, dogs, cats, maids, cooks, golf clothing, yachts, boats traveling across the Sound to party on Friday Harbor, and I picture my own childhood, running along the bluff with the neighborhood children, causing havoc and energy to be displaced and barely remembered. When young, the summer months pass with unremarkable pleasantness. All wishes are there and revealed, visible, kind, promising as well. Parents are supposed to grant them, the needs, and sometimes the yearning wants.

There's a knock on my front door. For a second I think it's Jo who's independently changed her mind about staying here for a few more days to support me, but when I open the door I see Margo and Anna standing outside—the police kept us for so long the night before, Jo slept over and left in the late morning. Who else could run the store? Margo and Anna aren't smiling, and I'm wondering about work, and who the college will get to substitute my classes, it's always a game of catch-up, and Roadway, who has nuzzled up to the storm door to get out; the police, who say they are canvassing the neighbors about the threats, which will only make these same neighbors vigilant and suspicious of me, start neighborhood watches to comfort me, and never let me forget the strangeness of the event, bring it up from this moment forward: remember when someone was stalking you? No harm no foul, right? Margo looks pushed in, a woman who is losing her family home to the bank, dressed in a short black jacket over a white blouse and jeans. Anna's arms fling forward when she speaks out, "Patrick, can we come in?"

I try to lighten the mood by laughing, and saying, "Middle of the night skullduggery. I forgot that you two knew each other." The words fall flat and I duck my head as I open the door for them. Roadway stares up and limps out onto the porch, but I catch her quick and shoo her back in. She hisses and moves into the shadows down towards the master bedroom. She won't venture out of the room again. I've pissed her off and she always pouts by giving me the silent treatment. Besides, Roadway isn't a social animal. I flip on more lights. Dim them down a bit.

Anna speaks again in the hallway and she reminds me of my high school geometry teacher,

Mrs. Cortez, who used her arms, hands, to punctuate the theories, the many different shapes, triangles, rhombuses, trapezoids, dancing fingers, the looseness of shirts stretched when she spoke. "We came here to apologize to you." I hear this and my heart tightens with nervous energy. I don't feel relief.

"Let's go into the living room." I always have to play the perfect host, even at unexpected times. One thing my mother did teach me. As we walk down the short hallway, we pass dozens of family photographs I couldn't take down when the house became my sole property: The Whidbey Island Summer Fair, Jobeth at the top of the King Slide, 30 feet in the air, ready to come down, smiling with fright and wonder. This is well after we first moved into the Anacortes cottage, when my parents loved each other without having to think so deeply about it, when father was on the verge of making it as a land developer, a big time real estate operator, buying up beach lots, miles of coastal shore, selling at one time for loads of money, making someone happy or not, helping kick them out onto some weary street, the roll of the lucky dice before the last economic bloodbath, but my father paid peanuts for the land, and this level of public business helped my mother feed her cravings, portray a proper image to the people of the town, the political power of reputable addresses on the island, always wanting more and more, and I could never will myself to measure up, become more than a sharp thorn.

A snapshot of all five of us in front of Father's new boat, "Little Connie"—Constance, Jobeth, and Patrick, pinned in tight between Mother and Father, and, in the old photo, Constance holds Mother's hand like a lifejacket. I wonder who took the photo; some drunker friend of Father's who was there for the celebration, the boat launch.

I remember my little sister drowning, but not who was supposed to have been watching her—and I confess right here that I've been lying to you—of course I remember who mother placed in charge of watching Connie. She's still here in the house; I can feel her, not old enough to read, forever, loose straw-yellow hair to match Jobeth's, spiraling into the water, and I keep telling myself it wasn't my fault—another lie. I've become such a talent at seeding these untruths. Should I take the blame? I was on the boat, too, that day. Can I ever pay that debt? Is the silence always going to be my sentence? The cold, calculated stare from my mother (did she see?), the empty arms drawn back to swing and strike? People move on and on. My parents grew apart and misery filled the house, dust in the corners of the cottage, abandoned doghouses, ivy growing up the far side, the Eastern side, and the neighbors talking about the cruelty of it all, the wreckage within the house flaking the paint off the windows, doors, and walls, inside and out, the upkeep, the damage being done to the rest of the family, and my mother spitting the blame, hitting me with the abandonment.

How can I accept any offered apology? Haven't I been taking too much from those around me? Can I listen to Anna and think of my family without telling her I'm also sorry and ashamed?

"I'm sorry too," I say, "I know you're friends of Wendy's. What I did was really shabby—I wasn't myself. I shouldn't have called Wendy's the other day, but I wanted to apologize. You were right to berate me. I did do enough to Wendy." Margo and

Anna sit on the peony-print couch side by side. They can't look at each other.

Margo appears flat, yet earthquake-proof, her hair jots off in different directions. I ask if I can get them a drink. They choose a simple red table wine I always keep handy. To calm my nerves I also pour myself a glass.

"We know what you've been going through lately. We wanted to watch your face when we told you."

"We felt that you should get what you deserve." There's power in Margo's statement as if hidden energy peppers her body from within. I've never seen her this way before. In the office she's always a totem, seldom there, but transfixed by the paper mill of student writing, the thankless job of making sense out of dangling participles. Beneath all that I see such rage. This woman hates me with every fiber of her being. There's tightness in her jaw, her lips are thin and each word she speaks hurts.

"It started like a joke, something impractical, something we've never done before in our lives. Once it got started we couldn't stop; Wendy was hurting so much, but now even that doesn't matter." Anna glances at Margo, who is slivering her nails, twisting a cuticle.

I remain silent; I know what they're talking about; there's something else though, the drunken, slow mannerisms, the disheveled clothing, Anna's red swollen eyes betray something more.

Margo says, "You seemed so aloof, and when Anna told me about what you did to Wendy, I wanted to teach you how to treat women with respect. I'm sorry too, now, truly sorry." She starts to cry, softly, quietly, a woman in an old silent movie.

"I don't know what to say. If I'm understanding you correctly, your actions mystify me. I need to think about this for a while. You both need mental help, and that's me being polite." I say this with a harsh undertone though. I've never been successful at channeling threats verbally. I wonder if I'm connecting anything together. These two women made the bomb threat? They made the doll. They threatened me. Anna of the spidery script.

"We didn't mean to push you any further than you pushed Wendy. What you did was cold, heartless. All she talked about was how you left her.

She was telling you about her mother's death and you deserted her. You embarrassed her. It affected her gravely." The word makes her cough. "The three of us wondered how you ever grew up, where you learned to disregard women?"

We sit across from each other, testing the stress, the poisoned oasis between us. I feel betrayed. "You threatened me and my sister, everyone at the restaurant. All those people you hurt with your thoughtless trick."

"We wanted to show you the same courtesy." This from Margo, whose features become unforgiving once more, less frayed, more the normal (normal equating a bitter scar from yesteryear driving Margo's actions), everyday-schoolmarm Margo. She looks at Anna as if waiting for permission to continue, to drop the ball or practice a sleight-of-hand trick. Anna nods, as if giving the final okay. *I'm with you. There's no turning back.*

"You know I could press charges. Turn you in. Call the police right now."

"Do it." Margo says, and with scary venom attached. "We'd deny everything, and, besides, it doesn't really matter anymore."

"Try denying it was your handwriting on the notes. The police have them. I'm surprised they haven't visited you yet—they're doing that, you know, calling all of Wendy's friends. You don't think. Both of you. I can't believe this." My tone, heavy with scorn, rises, as I try to be scathing. I see Margo's shoulders slump, rolling forward.

I look into Margo's eyes, blue, flecked with gray specks, intersecting red spots. I have to share my office with her. At the end of my vacation I'll put in for a transfer, lock myself away from this woman, someone who can act so caring about the box with the punctured doll, someone who probably picked out the wrapping paper and helped Anna wrap it up. Behind them, I see the back of their heads in the wall of mirror, and their heads are smaller, the hair wilder, matted and feral. Margo keeps pulling her flouncy white sleeves over her wrists, and this irritates me even more.

"I think you should leave." I stand and turn to lead them to the front door, expecting them to follow me. When I reach the hall entranceway I know they're still sitting on the couch, drinking their wine. I go back. I cannot figure out what to do next.

"We want you to listen to us, Patrick." Anna is holding onto a small clutch purse. "Please." She's added an earnest friendliness to her tone. She's a good actress. "I want to put this behind us. Joseph doesn't know anything about what happened, yet, and you're both still good friends. Please. Listen."

"What's your connection?" I stare at Margo, who juts her chin out and flicks her fingers across her shoulder, rubbing an ache.

"I'm a friend of Wendy's. She and I go back a long way. I feel responsible for the whole thing. She and I were going to start an online business together. I also have contacts in the print galleries down in Bellevue." She's talking like an android, listing pat memories. I didn't know Margo thought of herself as an artist. There's a tear forming in her eye and I feel weak in its presence.

I don't know what Margo does outside the office. I guess I never really cared. She probably told me, but I wasn't listening. She's so steady, so independent—someone I thought knew the difference between reality and illusion. Why didn't I talk with her more?

Before I can say anything, Anna speaks; she's fastidiously clear, and the world tilts; I feel a weight pressing me down into my chair again. I don't know how to reply. She says, "Wendy killed herself this afternoon."

I hear Wendy telling me she's afraid to die, how she wonders what it's like and isn't this all there is? I stutter my words and I know Wendy's image, like Constance's, will haunt my dreams, my waking world forever more. I say, "How?" The word comes out short, cold. I'm the only one alive who knows how Constance drowned in Puget Sound, tumbling off the boat so long ago now in the past. How many times do I have to lie about it?

She didn't fall. Constance rolled into the cold water because I pushed her, what brothers, siblings, do every single day. She hit her head on the sharp edge of a fishing tackle box. And she died there. I looked around and no one saw this. I rolled my sister into the deep. I wiped a spot of blood off the deck with a rag and threw that into the water as well. I took my punishment for years. But now? I see. My mother was there. She watched the whole thing from the back window of the boat's cabin, her hair a frizzy halo, her mouth an open wound. Constance's body drifted away, sunk a bit, and my father couldn't find her, circled the boat for hours in that area. Of course I worried about being found out, what my mother would say. Her small, broken body washed up on an island only visited by sea kayakers weeks later after circling, dipping, journeying through dark waters. She fell and must've struck her head.

I remember listening to my mother speak to my father the next day, "When they find her, there'll be hell to pay." They were in the kitchen, pouring drinks.

"Shut up. Not another word."

I sat on the stairs with Jobeth. She whispered, "What did you do?"

"Nothing."

"We should send him away. Find a boarding school, a military camp to shape him up, fix his problems."

"What did I say? If you bring this subject up one more time . . ."

"Patrick?"

"What?"

"I won't let them send you away."

"I won't either."

"Two policemen visited Wendy this morning and asked her a lot of questions about you and all the stuff Anna and I did, the restaurant, the telephone calls. Wendy sounded not herself, strange when she spoke to me on the phone after the policemen left. I could tell she knew everything even though I didn't tell her." Margo stands up, walks over to the end table and pours herself more wine. "Wendy got into her car and started the engine after setting up a garden hose. A neighbor found her." She drinks the wine down in two swift gulps and then places her glass next to the wine bottle, wipes her hands together as if they need washing, and remains standing there—bereft.

Wendy spoke about her own mother's death in that same way: mechanical, detached, did she know the train was coming, did she fight to get out of the car? Do any of us ever see how far back the train is?

I scan the phrases I remember Wendy spoke, try to find any hint, any clue to fathom the reason why. Was she really hurting that much and was I wearing blinders? Am I to blame? The doll, a simple message, and the hatpin skewered through the ears; if I pull the pin out will I be able to listen?

There's nothing more I want to hear. "Are you telling me it's all my fault?" Defensiveness creeps in, and I sound so pathetic. I am not to blame here. A new conversation must begin with these women, but I can't help myself. There is so much I want to say. I can't believe what these two women have told me. "I hope you can live with what you did."

They're both tearing up in unbearable silence (for the past, perhaps, and for what they came here to do), and I feel reactionary tears in the corner of my own eyes; they come unbidden—these are tears of anger, uselessness, blame I'm familiar with because it's always questionable—I will not beg for mercy. Anna's face is pinched and I know she's the only one here for absolution; she's following Margo's lead. Margo takes Anna's arm and pulls her to her feet. Anna nods again, giving permission, strength to do what they've planned all along—I get this now—I welcome it. We face each other, the conversation scarring bleach marks on dark wool. We stand there only a short time, an eternity—seconds. I perceive their judgment, their own complicity, in their complicated expressions. Is Anna about to begin blubbering? Either that, or she's one of the best actresses on the island. I can't help it when I step forward with my arms stretched open to encircle them, pull them close to me, which they allow, Margo's instinctual revulsion shown only by a facial tick, her lips twitching into grimace and then straightening into a horizon-less line—my operating instructions take over and I'm once more willing to listen to every sound they make—the silent son.

I can't help it.

I hear my mother's bile-filled voice echoing forth from the dark corners of the house: *Yes, you can, Patrick.*

I want to scream.

I don't say another word, not even when I see Margo's reflection in this house of mirrors pull out a short, sharp, wicked boning knife from beneath her billowing shirtsleeve, and raise it above my back. Anna ducks under and away from my arm and holds my right hand with both of hers—I can't tug away or escape her clutches. I'm staring into Margo's eyes when she plunges the knife in and I feel her fury. I watched this train as it headed right for me. I didn't move from the tracks. I don't know why. My feet fumble out from under me, and I fall, grasping, hanging onto both of them. I don't feel the knife as Margo jerks it out of me again . . . and again.

THE END

I hope you enjoyed reading my very first Horrorstruck novella. If you would like to read more of my work, please check out the twelve dark tales collected in Sandcastle and Other Stories, realistic holiday tales in Hark: A Christmas Collection, and my first psychological crime novel, Wake Me Up. All are available from Amazon, exclusively.

Now, please enjoy a short story original to this collection, The Night, a tale of small island town Washington and a parent's fear when one of her kids is late coming home.

Following that is a Bonus short story from Sandcastle and Other Stories, On the Back Staircase, a tale of a young girl dealing with a strong case of night terrors one long dark Ohio evening of yesteryear.

THE NIGHT

You are a child of nine living on an island in the Pacific Northwest. The summer heat is a stranger here, and approaching nightfall chills the air this close to Puget Sound. Laughter from the internet, a video being shared, wafts upstairs, mother watching cooking show bloopers and disasters while speaking to her best friend, Yvonne, from Seattle's nearby Mercer Island. She has a full glass of chardonnay, and isn't even thinking of you or her other son.

There are two children in the home that built this family of four. Father is away visiting his uncle down on Camano Island, a planned "boys night out" all on its own. His motorcycle is gone—and father relishes these hour-long rides, often taking the farm back roads to Conway, racing the Snow Geese. It's now so close to twilight, the Sound sunset clinging to Lopez Island in the distance, and your brother isn't home yet and all the rules your parents list blink and fill up your thoughts. He's only eleven, brainier than you'll ever be, more sensitive, enlightened for his age, more thoughtful, and cunning in an admirable way. And seen as responsible, trustworthy enough to follow the golden rules, once given permission to join school pals later in the evening at the school playing fields—not talking to strangers, not abandoning your friends, coming home in a group and on time. You hope to join the same ultimate Frisbee gathering in a few years—or maybe you'll choose little league, forge your own path separate from your older brother's chosen sports.

Even with the natural bickering that develops between siblings, sons, you and your brother are seen as sweet children, praised by most adults, friends of the family, acquaintances, strangers who can't keep opinions to themselves. They are observed in crowds, but no more than any other family.

It's an end of summer night. The first day of school looms ahead, closer now, near August's final curtain call. Mother wants to take you shopping for school supplies, un-scuffed jeans, a few shirts that you'll stuff behind older clothes in your closet, the one your mother thought would double as a reading nook, painted in silver, white, black, with red knobs, to resemble the inside of a fantastical spaceship, adding a bench with painted-on seatbelts, gears to turn, universes to conquer.

At the slightest hint of a chime from a distance down the street, a playful tune entering the open window, you race down the stairs and ask your mother if you can have a chocolate pop.

"I finished all my peas. I can bring you a real fruit bar."

"It's all you think about—ice cream." She says this as an aside under her breath. You're too young to understand what passive or aggressive means. The jabs a parent makes will build up into a wall of bitter foundation if this was a fairy tale. You don't think this. It's there in your mother's worry—what will happen, if . . .

"Please, mom. I promise to be quiet."

"I wanted to wait until your brother came home, for dessert." What will happen if he's lost? For good. "Where is he?"

After dinner, your brother joined two buddies of his halfway across town. These two pals are the ones who hang on his every word, tease you whenever no adults are around, mercilessly, and often jovially, including you in their games when they need a fourth, a spare. A summer Ultimate Frisbee league took over your brother's Tuesday and Thursday evenings on the middle school's open field above the six public tennis courts.

They'd play for hours if possible, and you aren't worried by your brother's late arrival. Yet. You get alone time with your mother, who is pacing the kitchen. You help her with the dishes, scolding the family dog, Finnegan, Finn, away from licking the leftover Shepherd's Pie made with ground turkey, carrots, peas, and mashed yams on top instead of Yukon Golds. You hear your mom speak to her girlfriends about dieting habits, the best wines (your mother is an expert), and always, eventually, carbs. These remain a mystery, a negative in your mind. You love potatoes, but they're bad, along with soda, and bread, and it's a wonder ice cream is still an offered dessert.

Your mother gives in as the chimes of the ice cream truck turn the corner on K Ave, blossoming.

"Get me a fruit Popsicle, Lime if he has any left, please, and two of whatever you decide. Your brother can eat his when he returns from frisbeeland."

"He's never been this late before. It's almost full dark." You don't know why you felt compelled to say this, twist some invisible knife. The look of wincing pain on your mother's face turns her smooth features ugly.

"You don't worry either. I'm not. Now scoot or you'll miss him." She hands you ten dollars.

You scoot. Out the back door and down the alleyway separating the in-town homes from one another, garage bays placed in the rear, out of sight, the front façade designed to capture the Puget Sound view, and up a slight rise to the corner of 7th and K right in time to make the ice cream truck stop. Another neighbor and his daughter approach from the other side of the street, money in hand, laughing carefree. She's an only child, younger than you are. Her needs are met.

"Good evening, young Sir!" says the ice cream man, "I'll always stop for the last customers of the night."

"I'd like three. One lime fruit Popsicle and two Fudge Bomb Bars." You add please at the end and the ice cream man makes change with your ten-dollar bill before handing over three wrapped treats.

"Enjoy the sweetness now. And this night."

You don't say anything else, run straight back to your home, as if the night, darkening, colors and then transforms everything into a scarier place. You don't know the word ominous yet. You learn what it means when you overhear your mother using the word as you hand her the change and her lime Popsicle. Your brother's treat goes onto the freezer door shelf.

"I don't know. He should be home by now. What did Richie say? He's not back either? I hate to jump to ominous conclusions. That's not like me. My intuition is stressing me out. That's all. Call me when Richie returns. I'll call Everett's parents." Your mother disconnects.

Standing behind the front corner window you see the lights across to Guemes Island, the ferry making a return crossing, an island neighboring Fidalgo Island. Close enough to your 6th St. location that you can see people bicycling on sunny days with a good pair of binoculars. You pretend these people are ants as you finish your chocolate dessert without making a mess.

Most of the living room is white, off-white, slipcovers in contemporary shades of sand, desert, muted bronzes, with artistic lighting features—your mother spent three months renovating, re-flooring, repainting—out with the old, in with the new. It's a quaint historic house, a cottage from the 1920s, with three small bedrooms up the stairs on the second floor, one with a front-facing balcony big enough to stand upon, but with a low railing that makes the deck a forbidden zone for you and your brother.

"We better go look for Miles. Parker, wash your hands and we'll take Finn for a walk." Finn wags his wiry tail and bounces like a pogo at the sound of his name. He tends to nip when excited and mother sours whenever she has to leash him. Her forearms are dotted with blemishes from Finn's nipping and she needs to talk to your father about finally training Finn to be calmer.

You find yourself on a new adventure. In your mind, the world darkens and grows lush with jungle vegetation; the Madrona tree-bark peels and curls in front of you, reaching. Your mother's voice is strained, and you do what she says. She bought you a treat, after all, and all the melted chocolate on your hands whirls down the powder room sink.

"Can I hold Finn's leash?"

"Sure. Miles will love to see Finn." Finn is most excited to see Miles each day when separated, when Miles returns from school.

Hooking the leash to Finnegan's collar is easy. The dog is six months old, a black, white, and tan, wiggly cattle dog mixed with some kind of mid-size poodle, and you hold on tightly. For after dinner entertainment, Finn chases you and Miles around the dining room and the three of you have created a game of tag, where Finn seeks to touch you by the time you return to home base, a chair in the living room—one loop around the dining table and back— Finn happy, darting and barking, taking shortcuts under the table and between the dining chairs, and you two brothers laughing icicle laughs, sparking more giggles from your parents as they watch the spectacle from the living room couch—a family.

"I wish your dad was home." Mother says this with some gravity. She's in a serious mood, and she locks the back door.

The two of you, with Finn circling, walk down the alleyway to the street, repeating your earlier steps to the ice cream truck. It's full dark now, and you imagine the world shrinking, the jungle adventure fading away. The air isn't chilly, yet, and that will come soon enough this late August. Island air conditioning.

"Miles. Miles! We're walking up K Avenue." Your mother yells this out and you cringe. Miles isn't lost. You feel this. But then a stray thought says: what if he is?

"Maybe they stopped in Causland Park on the way home," you say, "We go there all the time with Finn and Dad."

"But never alone and this late at night." You can't see the worry on your mother's face.

If your father was home, he'd drive down the Avenues on his motorcycle, the one that looked like it came right out of the fifties, a black, chrome, and white dream of a machine. Even this makes you think of death, the concept so forbidding. You know what death is. Hamsters died and went off to the backyard to be buried in shoeboxes. A Great Aunt died years ago, lived into her nineties, drank beer every single day. When Miles grows up, he says he'd like to do that too. Live to a hundred and drink beer every day. They didn't know this Great Aunt well, never met cousins from that family branch because of a long-buried rift, but your favorite Aunt gave the news gravely one wintery morning when you were too young to grasp the concept of death. The first hamster pet followed the next year.

When they moved into the house they heard the story of one of the former owners, the family previous to the sellers, from a friend of a friend at a fourth of July barbecue. This pal had spent most of her childhood playing with the daughter in the same house as kids living in town over thirty years ago.

"Can you believe it? I love that house. You're so lucky they accepted your offer. I know all about it!" This friend's enthusiasm lit up the gathering as she remembered bright childhood moments, and then everyone knew.

Motorcycles. This became the signpost. A dark coincidence.

"He isn't going to ride his motorcycle that much. He may even sell it." Your mother protested with such defensiveness and said this to her friends to stave off judgment, to help quench a sparking anxiety within her heart every time your father decided to spin down to Camano Island. Your mother liked motorcycles, snowmobiling, roller coasters at the fair.

You listened to the story. Death. Accidents. These tales fueled curiosity and frightened you. Fairy tales did the same.

"Well. The family moved in. There were three kids, an older girl in the smaller bedroom and twin boys in the larger upstairs room with bunk beds. It was a different era. We played together all the time. I'm still friendly with Cherie. She lives in Baltimore. Married with her own set of twin girls. Not two years after moving into the house, their father died in a motorcycle crash. It was the saddest moment in town for a long time after that. Cherie's mother worked at the refinery. They lived in the house until the kids graduated high school; she remarried and moved to Portland once the house became an empty nest. Cherie said she might return for the high school reunion. I can't wait to tell her I know the people who live in her old house."

Death.

By motorcycle. Two sons and a daughter. A family of five . . . and then four. Could four become three?

Fate can't be that cruel. Lightning striking twice. Burning. You think about fate in the simplest of terms while Finn sniffs the edge of the sidewalk and your mother decides to turn left to cross Causland Park off her search list. She's thinking of meth heads, the few homeless people she sees begging for food outside the markets, and terrible fates. Why did she let Miles join? She could go pick him up, take the time, keep him safe.

She calls out for Miles once more and then studies a text from Richie's mother.

Kids not back yet. Worried!

Sent Bud out to the field but they aren't there either. He's driving the Avenues there to home.

Your mother replies: *walking to Causland Park!*

You cling to your mother, hand her Finnegan's leash. You don't want her to die. You don't want anyone to die. Why are your thoughts so filled with doom? When father gets home, you don't want to see his face fill with thunder and follow strict orders to go to your room—to heavily think about what happened that evening.

The park looms ahead in the darkness. The city replaced the public lights with bright LED bulbs but the moonless quality darkens the park's interior. You hear the wind begin and the heat of the day lessens. It's just a breeze, but your imagination quickly turns it into a maelstrom. This park is made of old coastal stone embankments, designed with a pattern of lighter and darker stones, to form a natural theater. Bands and lectures gathered there, outdoor theater, actors performed there during town events. The trees stood tall, most over a hundred years old, shadowy ferns at their feet, lots of places to hide. Your mother's thoughts go to this place and she steps into the park and stops, thinking about who is concealed within. Waiting. What if Miles and his friends came through the park, stuck to the pathways, and fell prey regardless of how much they talked to him about not talking to strangers? She overheard another mother at the library just the other day whispering about how this area has many missing children, several each year, gone without a trace.

There are small towns across the country just like this one. Kind, gentle, neighbor-loving towns by day transformed into dark, scary, drug-busted monster-filled caricatures of themselves by night. You hear your mother talk all the time about drug users, how the police catch them at night, only at night, doing sketchy things closer to town when the bars close.

The night insects, crickets (Jiminy!), stop chirping. The birds are asleep in their nests. The park grows forbiddingly closer.

"Miles?"

This shout is weakening.

The entrance to the park becomes darker than everything else around it. Tense with foreboding. Oh, it's so dark. You squeeze your mother's hand tighter. Finn is stuck to your side, shivering.

There's only silence. The streets are empty. There are no cars moving, even in the distance of the downtown street. You imagine these other towns just like this one becoming ghost towns.

We're so far away from everything. At this moment.

Mother bites her lip.

Finnegan tunes to your fearful vibe and almost wraps around your legs with the leash and trips you to the sidewalk. It's so dark. He's too anxious to bark, but he lets one alarming yip escape.

The silence grows. You don't want your mother to call out again. Now it's the entire park that fills with an ominous tension. You think of the word ominous. Finnegan tilts his head towards the tree limbs sketching their own patterns in the layers of darkness. You know something is about to happen. You can feel this and you take a step backwards, pulling at your mother's hand. She feels your fright.

You think of the land beyond this island resting in dreadful slumber. The world at rest and everyone with closed eyes. Lights blinking on and off around the globe. You see this globe spinning and the names of countries, the ones you know, appearing. You see the sliver of orange glow from the distant oil refinery now materializing above the trees, an island presence, combatting the darkness of the night.

She does call out then. Again. This time with a fearful note added to her adult, softening, mothering, and worrisome lilt. There's nothing wrong here. You think this.

Bad things can't happen to you or anyone in your family. This is a repeating thought in your head.

You hear a twig snap ahead of you and Finn barks at the sound.

From across the park: "Hey, Mom? Coming!"

It's Miles.

"We're here!"

The silence breaks and you hear sneakers padding, running across the sidewalk slicing through the park, approaching.

The dark retreats. After being faced with such an ill-mannered moment, it begins to gather strength once more from its mercurial place. The nerve of some people. The stars begin to pop back into being. They were always there. Look what fear can do? The power.

The night insects begin to sing again as the three kids pile out of the park, laughing and remembering the high points of their Frisbee game. Your brother Miles, Richie Bontiger, and Everett Carmichael, push their bikes, giggling.

"Hi, Mom! Hi, Parks! Hey! We had to walk all the way. Richie's bike went flat!"

"Like his brain," says Everett, the smallest of the three boys, the one with red hair as dark as fire in the night.

"Miles, you are going to get such a talking to," declares your mother. "Richie. Everett. Your parents are waiting for you." The three boys mumble goodbyes and separate, go on ahead. The fear is gone, vanquished in another moment. Your mother feels this. It will remain there in her head, her heart, forever. Your mother texts that she found the boys safe and they're on their way home right now. None of the boys had cell phones, and this is another worry. She's been resisting the gift of a cell for Miles, the oldest. Now, she'll have to rethink that, another conversation to have with your father. She's seen other kids with cell phones and how they take over, how kids become glued to that small screen. The kids are all right. Nothing bad happened to them. They were laughing. A cell phone wouldn't have changed the night.

As you walk back with your lost and found brother, you're glad he's alive. For a moment there, you thought—

You hand your brother Finn's leash. Your mother takes charge of your brother's bike. A flat tire is something you'd never seen before and this brought excitement rather than frustration. You learn something new.

In the distance and over the hillside towards the far marina you hear a foghorn. In the morning this fog will creep in and then dissipate in the dawning heat.

You go to bed earlier, when your mother tells you to, without complaining, shivering as if a ghost steps over your own grave, in the bedroom that used to house twin boys long ago, your brother a room away, drifting to sleep listening to the sound of the foghorn as well. You're thinking of this Great Aunt who died of pneumonia late in the evening, years and years ago, and beer, how awful it tastes.

You can smell the Sound. It's magic. You stop shivering.

Earlier, you hear footsteps on the walkway towards the back of the house when you return home. A man clears his throat and you know him, you've heard this before. It's familiar.

Mother says, "That's your dad."

And so it is.

THE END

(AFTER RAY BRADBURY)

ENJOY A DARK TALE FROM:

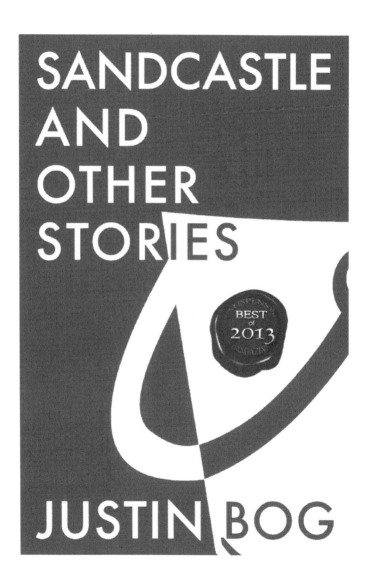

ON THE BACK STAIRCASE

The red farmhouse is dark. In one of the four upstairs bedrooms, Anna keeps waking up, restless, unnerved, making up stories in her head. God. It's so dark. And, finally, she can't bring herself back to sleep anymore. Is this one of those dreams where the dream is so real you wake up feeling like you've worn out the whole day already? Anna hopes not because this dream or this reality is scaring her.

Anna spent the last two hours lying on her bed, under two heavy blankets, staring out the cold, splintered casement window at the stars. By design, the window opened like a door right over the front porch roof; in case of fire, the family would escape with a ten-foot leap down to the ground, without thinking of broken ankles, legs, for very long, but Anna couldn't think of anything else. The stars in the chilly night sky moved, twirled into new shapes, like cloud watching after waking from a deep sleep when the clouds acted out your dreams.

Two hours ago Anna heard three locks fasten as the rest of her family went to sleep, her parents coming up last to make sure Jeff and Alan were really in their proper bunk beds and not throwing pillows at each other. The boys' door was locked from the inside; no fighting sounds could be heard so Anna's parents brushed their teeth, alternating spits of Crest into the shell-shaped basin.

Her parents always end up doing their nightly rituals together. They're never apart, as if they are the twins. They even teach art at the same university, and share a large painting studio.

After switching the bathroom nightlight on, which gave off a warm condensed-orange glow, Anna's parents shuffled into their bedroom down the hall. Anna heard their slide-bolt click and a spontaneous burst of laughter from Mom, then, distinct, even if a bit hushed: "There's a rip in your boxer shorts." Anna pictured Mom getting a needle and thread and fixing the tear while Dad still wore them. She knew that wouldn't happen and Anna listened intently to more giggling, and an hour later, light snoring.

The walls in the old, barn red, Victorian, rambling 1895 farmhouse are thin. It's 1981, and Anna wonders if they'll give their home a centennial birthday celebration, and then what the original family members who lived in the farmhouse were like.

A little while ago Anna saw something outside on the rural highway, large and slow moving. It started walking up the driveway, but then it vanished. One second it was there, a man-like form outlined against the whitewood fence separating Anna's house from her neighbors', The Smith's, modern ranch house, and the next second it's gone.

She knows she can't sleep now. She won't, even if she closes her eyes. Anna thinks: I'll keep watch. She imagines the dark man of shadow breaking in and slipping along the cool brown tile flooring of the kitchen, slowly sliding a knife, the one used to slice onions and bagels, out of the creaky drawer, and she listens for that creak.

Anna's so sure he's there that she scolds herself for scaring herself with her dreams, but, she thinks: what if there's a murderer down in the kitchen right now making plans? Who to kill first, whom to kill last, whom to make scream the longest. What will I do if he's skulking there? There's no lock on my door.

Maybe she should wake Dad to go check downstairs, but he has to teach his early class tomorrow, and it's almost 2:30 in the morning now. He'll be mad if this turns out to be another of Anna's late-night wolf cries. But then, he'll be mad if someone did break in, something he's always worrying about. Anna doesn't think her father could put up much of a fight against a maniac with dark ridges of muscle lining his forearms and chest; someone who stores up psychotic energy like a battery, who lives for destruction, a bloody rendering of the family unit, like the serial killer in that freaky new *Red Dragon* book her parents kept raving about and then tried to keep out of her naturally curious reach. Her parents loved scary books too. Anna had to sneak the Harris novel out of her parents' room to read little by little, captivated as she learned about the psycho who worked in a film development plant and chose his victims, entire families, by poring over their everyday birthday, Easter Sunday dinner, vacation photos: apple-pie families on picnics, brothers playing catch, sister and mother helping each other set the table for a special celebration dinner, father holding the new baby, staring into the camera, into the eyes of the killer.

Dad keeps telling his family: "The deadbolt on the front door is so flimsy, Ruby could've broken it down."

They reply: "Ruby's dead," which would stymie the conversation, but do nothing about fortifying the front door. Ruby was the first family pet, an old border collie mix who got hit by a car down the road a bit two years ago, but Dad would always bring her up when the family was all together in the same room because she hadn't been replaced yet.

Anna hopes her Dad wants a new pet for Christmas.

As Anna gazes at a dim star, she knows, deep down inside, she hasn't really heard anyone moving around downstairs, and she's wondering if she did see someone vanish on the gravel driveway. It could've been a cloud covering the sliver moon, a wind whipping October leaves into the bushes, maybe, but she also believes, down so deep now—I saw it—and she scolds herself anew—the shadow moving like an arm swinging by someone's side, someone strong, and muscled, and dark, clothes the color of night.

The star that barely blinks light reminds Anna of the orange bathroom nightlight one unlocked door away. Alan usually gets up in the middle of the night, stumbles to the bathroom, and forgets to flush, not because he's half-awake but because he always forgets. Dad hung a hand-painted sign on the bathroom door that reads: FLUSH FOR LIFE— as if the next time Alan forgets, he'd have no future and end up cleaning the bathroom for the rest of his life.

Turning into the kitchen, right near the back wall and the old white floor freezer, are the first steps of the back staircase. There are five steps, worn oak, taking you to a landing, a dark wider square space. The rest of the staircase steps branch to the left and lead you farther, up twenty-one steep steps to the second-floor landing. These wooden steps are painted eggshell blue to make the dark corridor lighter, but the color doesn't help brighten anything; the blue takes the light in, stores it up and makes Anna run down the stairs faster or take the front staircase.

After the man gets his knife and adds it to his darkening form he'd head for the first step, but he'd do it in his shadowy and sneaky way because Anna thinks he's aware now that someone upstairs is aware of him. He wants to do things carefully, make no mistakes.

The back staircase is next to the bathroom door, to the left once you reach the landing, and Anna's door is down from that maybe only ten feet at the turn in the corridor, which means Anna's bedroom door faces the back stairs. Before Dad bought the nightlight for the bathroom, Alan, sleepwalking, wandered out his bedroom door, to the right of the back staircase, and opposite the bathroom door. If this sounds confusing, try juggling for bathroom rights on every school day. Anna always beats her sisters into the shower, and they usually scream for Mom to get her to hurry up. Anyway, Alan walked out his door and must've thought he was going into the bathroom when, in fact, he was walking out into thin air. He fell down the slippery, painted, back staircase and broke his right leg in two places. Anna found him first, lying on the landing, because she always wakes up fast. Alan screamed there, injured and afraid of what happened and what was to come. Mom cried with him. Megan sat next to Jeff and Sandy, huddled at the top of the stairs.

Dad said, "Anna, go call an ambulance, dial 911." So she did, feeling pretty important. Alan's back was twisted in a funny position and Dad didn't want to chance moving Alan himself. Anna will always remember how her brother's face was lit up by scream after scream. By the time Alan came back home with a cast from thigh to ankle on his right leg, there was a nightlight in the upstairs bathroom. A cloud covers the star Anna's watching and she focuses on another, brighter one.

Then she hears . . .

A creak on the back staircase, and it's a sly one, as if someone's trying to sneak up, as if that someone wants Anna to hear that old creak. Or is it just the house settling? Thin walls? Either way, Anna won't go check and she thinks: Oh my God— anyway. Why do I insist on scaring myself?

Anna's twin sister, Sandy, the one she shares a room with, is asleep on the other twin bed across the bedroom, tucked under covers in the darkness. Anna says softly, "I heard something. Sandy, are you awake?"

Sandy only mumbles, "Shut up," and falls back into slumber. Anna is amazed at how quickly her sister departs to dreamland, as if a switch is flipped.

Anna thinks about the design of the house, wondering, keeping in mind the subtle shifting of weight she thinks she heard on the first wooden step. There are two staircases in the house. The first and main front staircase is covered with an old family runner, blood red, blue, aged-bone oriental carpet and the secondary back staircase, starting near the kitchen counter island, ancient wood. No one can ever sneak up on anyone, Anna, Sandy, Jeff, Alan, or Megan, using the back stairs. They can never sneak up on their parents, when they're cooking meals, either, but they do keep trying. They're a family made up of sneaks. All five kids are just at those ages, all of them yet to cross into their teenage years, but Megan's only a month away, and Sandy and Anna turn twelve in nine months.

Anna wants to remember, or keep in mind, that her family locks their bedroom doors when they go to sleep. Everyone except Sandy and Anna, who, out of sheer laziness, opted not to install a lock of their own; Anna feels that no one in her family is safe anymore, tonight. It's so late now and the moon has spun farther away, deepening the blackness of the driveway, where she won't see any shadow if it moved.

There's no lock on Anna's bedroom door. Sandy and Anna don't have an inside lock, a slide-bolt, or chain.

Once, Anna walked into the television room and asked for a simple hook and clasp: "Everyone else has one." But she didn't push for it.

Dad replied, not even listening to Anna completely, watching a PBS show with lots of poor static reception, "You'll have to install it yourself."

Anna's a very lazy person. She won't even clean her half of the room unless an extreme threat or blackmail is involved. Anna never thought she had a reason to push for a lock. Sandy and I never needed one before, she thinks, and besides, I like it when Jeff and Alan barge in demanding attention, wanting to play board games.

The others all had their own reasons for locks.

Anna starts to play a mind game. Instead of counting sheep, she sits up in bed with her back against the simple pine headboard and convinces herself that on this weekend October night she's the only person awake in the house, the only night owl up near this house, the only sleepless creature on the rolling yard, outside the Ohio town limit, where the television cable stopped three hundred yards from their house, right on the corner, and wouldn't come no matter how many calls to the cable company went through—the roof antenna bringing in scratchy versions of the three big networks, in Granville proper, the small university town, no one on campus pulling all-nighters, everyone still asleep, but, when awake, the people bicker about how the college kids drink too much at the #1 party college in the nation and whiz through town without a care, knowing their parents are footing the bill for their games, in sleeping Licking County, a half-hour drive to Columbus, where Dad and Mom drive the family to Chess King Malls, the JC Penney outlet store, where all returned merchandise finds a home, and Schottenstein's to try on discount clothing for hours, in what the

siblings call the silver cattle wagon, the youngest
twins yearning to sit in the way back reverse bench
seat so they can stare at the drivers of cars behind
them and make funny faces, every weekend to
escape the conservative, political, bureaucratic
yammering of the school administrators. In the
sleepy state of Ohio, where jobs have always been
scarce and businesses think the state is made up of
the finest cross-section of America and try to test
their products here first before setting up
nationwide, as if Ohioans like being guinea pigs, in
the United States of America, where the president
can fall down a lot and become the butt of jokes,
and the next president can be a peanut farmer and
become ridiculed for another reason, the new
president elected, to Anna anyway, acting as if he'd
just aced his session on a Hollywood casting couch.
Endlessly, in the Northern Hemisphere, Anna
imagines a continent asleep, everyone lying on cots,
in tents, on cold ground, in caves, and then around
the world, where natural disasters are the only
thing that binds the different, bickering countries
with penny-can compassion. But Anna's mind tires
of the game when she pictures the entire universe

asleep and how a big bang would wake it up, and then she thinks about how dark the hallway outside her door is and about the two staircases and all the locks. She tries to listen to Sandy's breathing. The sound is cool and low like a breeze in a field. As she listens, Anna tries to catch the sound of breathing outside the door on the back staircase, but she can't focus enough to hear anything.

Megan sleeps in a room around the corner, down the same hallway a short distance from her parents' room. With some relief, Anna ponders anew: if the man chose to kill the kids in order, Megan would be the first to go; she's the oldest. She has her own room. For privacy, Megan has an inner door lock. That's her reason. Once, Jeff crept in with a loaded crayon box and made his own celestial system, a purple, blue, orange and red galaxy, out of Megan's papers, books and posters. She needs the lock because of the door itself; it's warped badly and will never shut closed. Ruby would claw open Megan's door and hop onto her faded-rose comforter for a snooze, smelling up the room with dog. So a hook-lock was put on the outside also, and there are dog-clawing scratches as a Ruby reminder. Alan locked Megan in once for four hours when their parents were away and Megan was supposed to be babysitting the lot. Alan was grounded for two weeks. But Megan's inner lock would surely break under the shadow-man's thrust. The door would splinter on its Sears hinges and he'd rush in, knife held ready to swing forward in a curve. Anna can see Megan opening her eyes and looking into the darkness where the man's features should be, being swallowed up by the fear, the arm arcing down, and the cold blade slicing through her comforter.

Anna blows the image to smithereens by thinking about her younger brothers, fraternal twins, Alan and Jeff, how little safety their door lock is, how they're so much alike even though they're so far from identical. The monstrous man on the stairs hasn't taken another step—testing the night air even now, making his plans, will take another step soon, and Anna's waiting for the next creak. Alan and Jeff should be able to hear him coming because their bedroom is closest, but they're sound asleep after a full evening of kick the can with the neighborhood kids.

Alan and Jeff work in tandem, one prank after another. Jeff is the youngest of the family, by barely ten minutes, Alan breathing air first and squalling, waiting for his twin's cries to join in a chorus. They also share a room, but they have a lock on their door because they both whined loudly when Megan got two locks. They have other reasons too. They feel their things, Tinkertoys and Lego sculptures and comic books, are more important than anyone else's possessions, and should be kept behind locked doors. They like to sneak around in order to intrude in their older siblings' affairs; they have to be able to plan schemes behind closed doors. Sandy and Anna can't wait until they grow up, are constantly throwing the maturity word around when they learned it from Megan, when the boys will figure out how sloppy they are and clean up their act. With the lock issue, Dad put them on probation. If they abuse the lock on the door, he takes it off.

But they have a lock and because of that they're safe. Everyone would hear the man trying to break through their door, all the noise shooting throughout the house and walls, giving Mom enough time, even on the old black rotary phone in her bedroom, to dial 911, while Dad rushes out into the hall to confront the intruder. Anna fears for him and keeps quiet. She thinks: What if the man went after my dad first? What if I had no parents? She wouldn't know what to do then so she's happy for her brothers' safety from the sounds and anything making sounds on the back staircase. She pulls the covers up to her chin and listens. She knows the house and can see blueprints as if they're veins running across the back of her hand, floor plans as if they're right in front of her, glowing.

Every room has its own smell and every room makes its own creaks. Sandy and Anna have talked about these sounds and how they can tell when someone's in another room by the tread on the floorboards in the dining room or the squeak on the tile in the kitchen. Sandy can tell someone's coming up the back staircase because, she says, the creak sounds like a swaying, snapped sail on a wind-tossed ship. Sandy and Anna share their mother's melodramatic streak.

Sandy and Anna are also fraternal twins. Sandy, with a small, rabbit-y nose, dimpled chin, straw-blonde hair, looks nothing like her twin sister, Anna, who has dark curls Mom tries to straighten by brushing the heck out of them, and wide brown eyes to match. They're both pretty, and look nothing like Megan, who has a smattering of freckles across her straight nose, and new braces.

"You'll get them too," said Megan, "just you wait."

Everyone Anna's talked to jokes about the two sets of twins some way or another as if they must feel sorry for poor, poor Mom because she was so busy changing diapers or changing something else, trying to pick up one child without making the other twin instantly jealous. They talk about how different all five children look, how three pregnancies brought five babies into this world looking like individuals and not clones. They're amazed by this and laugh about the three different postmen who delivered mail on their street. Anna thinks people have to be cruel at times to hide their own insecurities. She admits being guilty of this from time to time.

Sandy and Anna don't dress in the same clothes, the same color. Even when they were born, they were different. Sandy was larger, louder, almost resentful, with a sharp analytical mind, and Anna was the quiet one with the expansive fascination, the one who always wanted to know why, what, who, and where first before placing all of the real facts into an imaginary landscape.

Anna listens hard for any sound coming from out in the hall and down the back staircase and thinks of dark twins, the good and the bad and she wonders if the man on the stairs has the same purpose, if he's really a twin in search of his lost twin. That would mean he's looking for Megan, that he isn't really a man at all, just a dark boy on the teenage cusp, and the image of Megan's door exploding, her twin rushing to join with her again in this world, makes Anna shiver, and she tries to count down from ten to calm her nerves. Megan's safe, Anna thinks. She has to be. Anna can't hear anything from the back staircase. And she goes back to thinking the intruder is once again a man, a destructive force. It couldn't possibly be a twin, a long lost member of her family.

Megan wanted a twin. Anna always wondered if she felt left out because of not getting one, until the day Mom told all the kids Megan showed some form of jealousy. Megan always protested mildly. You'd often find the family digging through their box of photographs. They didn't have an album. They had a large, sturdy, cardboard box. The photos Dad took are thrown in year after year and the box's corners are now taped together because it's handled so much.

A photo of Megan always surfaces; she's naked and splashing with glee in a yellow-duck-bordered baby pool in the early seventies, the sunlight shining in her eyes so no one can tell she has the darkest blue eyes of the family, as if they'd been painted with three extra layers.

Everyone laughs as the picture is passed around. Megan was a pretty baby, is a pretty child, and she knows when she's center-stage and loves the role.

A similar photo was taken, two years later, of Sandy and Anna in the same duck pool, not as bright, the plastic wearing thin and mud-smudged. Anna swears she remembers the photo being taken—Dad stopping them for a second, making Sandy and Anna look at the camera. Both had puzzled expressions on their faces, as if Dad were disturbing two military strategists planning battle. Anna swears she remembers going right back to pulling Sandy's hair, trying to dunk her head under as soon as the photo was taken, Dad intervening and yelling at Anna to stop being the way she was. Sandy always wins any physical fights they have; Anna's the one who gets dunked, but, nevertheless, Anna likes to instigate most of their battles. The verbal fights are a different story altogether, and the outcome is never certain enough to place winning bets.

And Anna's trying to fight sleep right now because she wants to hear the next creak, the next step and pretend it's really only the house settling, feed her imagination more. Because she believes someone's out there right now even though it's been minutes since the last settling creak. If this is real, if there really is someone out there, why is Anna just sitting in bed thinking of her past, her brothers and sisters, her parents, thinking about everything else but the man on the back staircase. Why can't she do anything?

She's scared and she's trying not to scare herself more, but her mind works that way. She pictures the night breaking into pieces and a light shining through the darkness falling and she wonders if she's dreaming because she remembers speaking to Sandy across the room. She wants to warn her about the man on the stairs coming up silently, almost silently. Anna opens her mouth to speak while pushing the covers down to her pajama-covered knees so she can step to the ground in one quick motion. And the lockless door bursts open and the grinning man with the knife comes in one step and tilts his head in Anna's direction and she's too scared to do anything but quiver and choke back screams. He rushes to her twin sister's bed and Anna can't move or protect Sandy in any way or protect herself because she didn't hide under the bed or in the closet when she had the time to do so. All Anna can do is yell, but she can't because she's awake. And she doesn't want to wake everyone else up, not just yet. Sandy would start shouting and whining at Anna in the darkness. Sandy wouldn't realize right away that her sister was watching over her, trying to protect her.

Megan always watched her two sisters fight, wouldn't break them up, as if she could care less if they tore each other apart, and if Megan's also listening to the man on the back staircase as Anna is, Anna wonders if Megan's hoping he'll go to her sisters' room first; Anna wonders if Megan feels safe behind her locked door. Anna would. As a matter of fact, Megan was also in the second photo, barely visible in the faded background, but there she was standing behind the pool near the picnic table. Watching Sandy and Anna fight.

When this photo is passed around Mom says Megan has always wanted a twin to fight with, play with, and belong to.

Megan always protests: "I did not want another me."

But her face reddens and she takes the snapshot and throws it back into the cardboard box. In some ways Anna's glad Megan didn't get a twin because she's always telling her younger siblings what to do, and everything she does is right and she doesn't have to be compared with anyone else. But in another way Anna wishes Megan did have a twin so they'd have a perfect set: three sets of different cufflinks. Dad and Mom liked to joke about cufflinks a lot, especially when they and their kids were younger.

The locks are important because Anna wishes to God Sandy and she had put one on their door when they had the chance. Now it's too late and the man is breathing silently on the steps, making plans. Anna can almost smell him, the scent of the woods he ran through to get to the highway and across the drainage ditch, the stench of the mildew and the dirt in the water on his pant legs, and Anna knows he really is there, waiting.

Anna was why . . . Anna was the reason why . . . what Anna did was the reason why her parents put a slide-bolt on their own bedroom door. Because she was so young and she didn't know what kind of sounds they were making and she really didn't care. All Anna knew was they were both home in one place and that she could tell on Sandy for ripping up the finger painting she made in third grade that day. Sandy shredded the construction paper on the school bus and Anna cried as she ran up the driveway, a curving hill, to her house, the same hill the man on the stairs crept up, passing like a shade over the bend in the driveway. Anna knew they were somewhere upstairs, her parents, because they weren't in the television room or the kitchen or the study and both cars were parked outside the garage filled with lawnmowers, rabbit hutches, still-unpacked boxes from the move to the country farmhouse life from their first in-town rental home on the other side of the incorporated line when they first arrived as a complete family from another university in Pennsylvania several years previously. So, Anna ran up the oriental carpet on the front staircase.

They didn't hear Anna coming. If she'd taken the back staircase, they would've had time to cover up. As it was, she stopped outside their door, shouted, "Mom!" and barged into the room. Her tears quit instantly and her eyes widened.

It was such a strange thing for Anna to see back then, the first time she put things together in her young mind. It was like . . . Anna had never really thought about anything like this before. Her parents had never gotten into the duck pool naked like Megan.

Then it was Mom's turn to shout, "Anna!" She dropped her ripped finger painting on their off-white shag area rug. It lay there forgotten until later when her parents sat them all down on the living room couch and explained something about locked doors. And more, in vague terms, privacy, concept, love, knocking before entering closed doors, openness, order and then orders that must be obeyed.

Anna said, "But your door wasn't locked, and Sandy tore my picture on purpose . . ." And she made tears come again to see what they would add.

That was enough to get Sandy in trouble, and was the only thing that mattered. Dad put a slide-bolt on his door the next day. But that was then, the images of her parents disturbed expressions, their bodies entwined, the sheets spread across the back of the bed and looping onto the floor, and they're all a little bit older, and even though Sandy and Anna like to argue, they do get along.

Anna's thoughts catch in her mind as the past second repeats itself; a little while ago she swears she remembers arguing, pleading with Sandy again. She whispered: "Please get up, get up Sandy, he's right outside our door, on the staircase." Anna turns her head and swears she can hear the breathing, smell the rot on his tongue and Sandy won't wake up, get up, so Anna doesn't wait this time and climbs out from under the covers and wiggles beneath her bed alone before the door shatters and bursts open and the grinning man comes in looking for two girls soon to become teenagers and finds only one. Inside, Anna tells herself it's the right thing to do, the only thing she could do to save herself. Sandy wouldn't wake up and listen to Anna and it's all her own fault, and she's sorry Sandy, and Anna's shivering on top of her bed again even though she's pulled the blankets completely over her head and she's in utter darkness scaring herself silly thinking how she let Sandy down.

Sandy and Anna have shared the same room, crib, Mom's belly, since whenever. Sandy's bed is closer to the door, next to the white splotchy-painted bookshelves. Anna's bed is on the other side of the room, next to one of the windows over the front porch roof, facing the highway and the

University's biological reserve beyond, the woods dark and chilling in the night's cold.

Anna remembers other restless nights, where she called out in the night and how Dad or Mom would come in and ask her if she was all right. The last time, only six months ago, when Anna was sneaking once more because of her age, after Anna saw that movie where all the babysitters end up slashed by a maniac who traveled through the night like a shadow, tinkling piano music drifting on dark wind, when she spent every weekend night babysitting and turning all the lights on bright until the adults came home, paid Anna for getting scared all alone in their strange houses, and drove her home late at night, her dark bedroom waiting for her, Sandy already asleep on her side of the room.

On some of these nights Anna would sneak out the window and crawl over the almost-flat roof shingles, hang her head over the roof 's edge. Thinking: it's only twelve feet down. She was on the front porch roof, which sloped gently, and she wondered if she could reach down enough to slide to the ground on the white pillars that held the roof up. But she knew her body wouldn't twist enough.

Then, once she knew she had no other choice, she'd pretend she was on the run. Anna had to jump, and she would in her mind. Without breaking an ankle, the fall would take her onto the grass and down the front hill, rolling all the way to the road. After she picked herself up, she'd be off.

And Anna knows she's thinking all of this when that someone on the back staircase takes another wicked step.

It sounds like a windblown rusty swing.

Halfway up now.

And if she's dreaming, Anna wants to wake up before the door bursts open again.

But she's not dreaming now and Anna's really scared herself this time because she swears she thought she heard another creak; the wind howling down the trees, and the windows shattering.

Sandy.

Wake up.

More than halfway up now.

And Anna wishes to God there was a lock on her door as she sits up in bed again, picks the blanket up by the edge, as silently as possible, and covers herself with it up to her eyes, the knuckles of her fingers hurting as they clutch the material. Swiftly, Anna drops the covers and opens the window to the front porch roof enough and sits back against the headboard. There're two more creaks on the back stairs, coming up faster now, and then another heavier sound as if that someone wants Anna to hear him stop three quarters of the way up, both feet on the same riser, and she's scared because Anna thinks he heard her open the window. Anna wants to warn Sandy, but she can't. He'd hear her and come faster, rushing through the only unlocked door on the second floor. And she stares at that unlocked door, then back at the open window, back and forth.

Wondering.

If she can make it onto the roof and jump for real this time without breaking her ankle, get to the neighbors before that someone becomes aware, the same someone who's almost to the landing now, who can see the door to this room straight ahead, who can see Anna through the door staring back at him, his face caught in the nightlight glow . . . Anna holds onto her covers tighter than before and listens for the next telltale step, and if she hears it, and if she hears anything else, she's out on the roof.

THE END

ACKNOWLEDGEMENTS

I thank my friends who have continued to share their love of writing in many different ways. Shari Ryan, Eden Baylee, Rachel Thompson, M.E. Franco, Barb Drozdowich, and Maria Savva . . . to my fellow dark writers out there in the field, please give me more tales to read!

Always a happy Thank You to Christopher James.

ABOUT THE AUTHOR

 Justin Bog makes his home in the Pacific Northwest with his partner of almost 30 years. He received an English degree from the University of Michigan, and an MFA in Fiction from Bowling Green State University. When not writing, he spends most of his time looking after his long coat German shepherd, Kipling, and two barn cats, Ajax The Gray & Eartha Kitt'n (she has a secret she wants to tell you). R.I.P. Zippy!

VISIT JUSTIN AT HIS A WRITER'S LIFE BLOG:

www.justinbog.com.

Follow Justin on Twitter @JustinBog.

You can also find Justin Bog's Author Page on Facebook:

https://www.facebook.com/JustinBog1.

Address: 1004 Commercial Ave, #480
Anacortes, WA 98221

You can email Justin at Justinbog@me.com.

Feel free to contact Justin through any of these communication routes and please let him know what you thought of **The Conversationalist**.

47902216R00104

Made in the USA
San Bernardino, CA
11 April 2017